Terror in t

Kendra woke at midnight with a gasp. The old house seemed to be breathing.

Inhale, exhale . . . inhale, exhale . . . the rhythmic sounds grew louder and louder.

Fear seized Kendra like an icy claw. Her throat tightened and her heart beat wildly. She couldn't control her terror.

And then she realized she wasn't alone.

THE TEMPTATION

MIDNIGHT Secrets

Volume I   THE TEMPTATION

WOLFF RYP

WESTWIND®
Troll Associates

PROLOGUE

You may be tempted to look for the house on 76th Street the next time you're in New York. But you won't find it. The huge, brooding mansion is set far back from the street in a cul-de-sac. It's so well hidden behind a high-rise building that passersby aren't even aware it exists. But it's there.

It sprawls on gloomy acres, overlooking the river as it has for centuries. Its wide terrace and shadowed gardens are deathly silent. The air inside its spiked iron gates is always chilled and stale. The sun never shines in the corner of the garden where the weathered tombstones of an ancient family cemetery huddle.

You'll only know the house is there if you spot the old, faded bloodstain on the sidewalk. Rain and snow have never washed it away. If you come there at night, you may see, in the faint glow of the streetlight, the bloodstain pulsing—luminous and shivering in the dark.

You may even see that it forms the letter *R*.

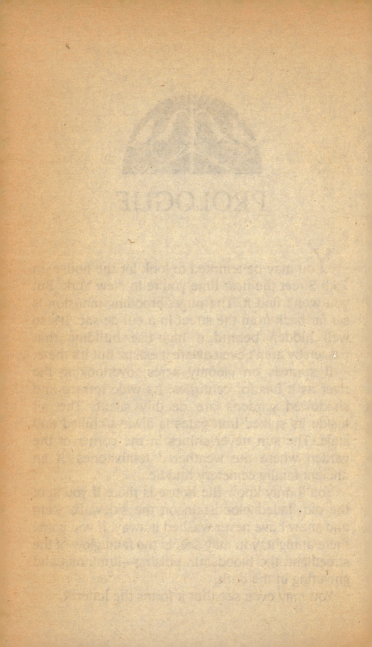

CHAPTER 1

Something is wrong. Terribly, horribly wrong.

She's lying in a box, a soft, cushioned box. She can see over its edge into a darkened room.

Is she in a coffin?

The thought almost chokes her with terror.

Then she realizes that she can move a little. If she struggles, she can wave her arms and kick her feet. She pushes with all her might to raise herself, but she can't.

Kendra opens her mouth to cry out. She must let them know she's not dead. She must tell them to get her out.

Someone, anyone, please come!

But she can't speak. No words will come. To her horror, all she can do is make soft, mewing sounds.

How will she let them know she's alive?

Everything around her is huge and seems to be growing larger every second. The shadowed room, the window opposite, the chest of drawers, the lamp with its dim light, the box she's in . . .

She tries to scream in panic.

Someone, come get me out of here!

But all she can do is gasp and utter those babbling noises.

Suddenly Kendra understands. She's no longer seventeen. She's an infant, only a few months old. Too young to speak.

The box isn't a coffin. It's her crib. She's alone at night in the bedroom she slept in when she was a baby.

But is she really alone?

Shadows from the light of the lamp are gathering in the corner across the room. They start spinning, faster and faster, moving toward her in a graceful dance. She hears a faint tinkling, like the sound of crystal chimes ringing in a gentle breeze.

The shadows are forming into a person—a slim, golden-haired man. He bends over Kendra and smiles at her. Fireflies of light swirl around his head as the chimes sing. He is the most beautiful sight Kendra has ever seen. She gurgles with joy.

The man lifts her tiny hand and kisses it.

"I am yours, and you are mine," he whispers. "I will come for you when you are ready."

Kendra stares up at him, hypnotized. His words are like music.

His voice starts to fade. "Someday . . ."

His body is dimming. "One happy day . . ."

He is gone.

✦ ✦ ✦

"No!" Kendra screamed.

She awoke, breathing in gasps, terrified. What had she been dreaming? She couldn't remember. She lay in her familiar bed in her cozy room, surrounded by the things she loved with all the passion of her seventeen years. She felt the familiar tingle of the rosy mark on the back of her hand. It was the birthmark her parents told her had appeared suddenly when she was only a few months old.

What had she been dreaming?

As she rubbed the tingling mark, Kendra began to shiver. That faint prickle on her hand had always been a warning. The message was always the same: Danger.

Something terrible was about to happen.

She struggled up in bed, trying desperately to control her panic. The tingle on her hand grew ever stronger.

Kendra, beware.

All her life, even when she was too young to understand its meaning, she knew the throbbing of the mark came before great danger. She felt its tingle as a child when she toddled after a ball straight toward an open window in her parents' apartment on the thirtieth floor. And when her pony, Duke, frightened by a snake, threw her to the ground and almost trampled her. And when she was about to board their boat with her father for that disastrous trip that sailed him into a sudden, raging storm. But something always averted sure disaster. Some force always saved her life. Her mother came into her room just as she was climbing out onto the window ledge and pulled her back. The whinny of another horse nearby distracted her pony, and he trotted off before he could harm her. She tripped on a coil of rope and hit her head as she fell to the dock, so her father took her back to the house and then sailed off alone.

And always she felt the same tingle on her hand just before disaster was ready to strike her down.

The fearful warning had happened many times before. But now the sensation was so strong it was painful.

Kendra! Danger!

Something about her dream. What was it?

What had she been dreaming?

As she rubbed her hand, Kendra was certain of only one thing: some unknown horror was about to come into her life . . . something powerful and ruthless . . . something far worse than anything she had ever known.

And she was unable to stop it.

CHAPTER 2

Kendra Linton threw back the covers and looked across the room at her sister.

"Are you okay?" Lauren Linton asked. She leaned against the door of Kendra's bedroom and fixed her older sister with a worried look.

"Yeah, I guess," Kendra mumbled sleepily.

"I heard you groaning as I was coming out of the bathroom. You're not sick, are you?" Lauren asked.

"No, just a bad dream."

Lauren came into the room and flopped down on her sister's bed. Her long blonde hair, still wet from the shower, trailed down her shoulders. She was frowning with concern. "Want to tell me about it?"

"I don't remember, but it was pretty bad." Kendra reached for the clock on her bedside table. She knew she had set the alarm last night. It was off now, but she didn't remember hearing it.

She yawned groggily, then shot straight up as she remembered that she was going to be late—on the most important day of her life. Today she was going to appear on live TV in her Communications class. Ever since she could remember, Kendra had wanted to be a broadcast journalist. This was the her big chance—and if she didn't hurry she'd blow it.

Kendra leaped out of bed, and her toe jammed into a thick math book on the floor. "Oh, no," she groaned as she stooped to pick up the book. "I've got a calculus test first period."

What was supposed to be the best day of her life was fast turning into the worst. And it had hardly even started yet!

"Do you want some help?" her sister asked.

"No, thanks. When I'm crazy like this it's better if I'm alone," Kendra said. She rushed toward the outfit she had laid out the night before, then stopped and stared at her sister. "Lauren, you've got blue gunk all over your face."

"I do? Ugh, gross! What is it?"

Kendra dabbed at a spot with her finger and said, "Chill out, it's just toothpaste. Get out of here and get yourself dressed. And no skipping breakfast."

"Yes, Mom."

Kendra smiled as Lauren ran out the door. At fifteen, Lauren was only a year-and-a-half younger than Kendra, but Kendra did feel like Lauren's mother at times. Since their father's death eight years ago, the girls' own mother, Dinah, was so wrapped up in her own world that the two sisters always turned to each other for support. Mr. Linton was drowned in the storm that swamped his boat the day Kendra just missed sailing with him. During the terrible weeks and months that followed, Dinah was completely self-absorbed. The girls grieved together and comforted each other. Now it was as natural as breathing. They were best friends. They did not have secrets from each other.

Kendra eyed the pale green blazer and matching green shirt that she had picked out to wear the night before and frowned. They would never work. She'd look like the Jolly Green Giant. What had she been thinking when she picked them out?

She threw the outfit down on her unmade bed and frantically began searching through her closet. She had to find the best outfit. Not too casual. Not too flashy. But perfect. Just like all her favorite TV news anchors.

"Kendra," Lauren said, poking her head through the door, "I'm leaving for school in five minutes, with or without you."

"Fine, fine," Kendra murmured from her closet.

After rejecting at least half-a-dozen more outfits, she finally settled on a soft, gray cashmere sweater with a short—but not too short for the camera—dark gray leather skirt. She was just slipping into the skirt when the doorbell rang.

"I'll get it," her sister shouted from the other room. "And then I'm leaving. See ya."

Half a minute later, Kendra's good friend Hallie Benedict pushed open the bedroom door. "Hi, Ken," Hallie said, her freckled face lighting up in a grin. Hallie's bright green eyes surveyed the clothing strewn all over the floor. "Whoa, what happened here? A bargain basement sale? I've never seen your room so messy."

Kendra and Hallie lived in the same Fifth Avenue apartment building across from Central Park—Kendra on the thirtieth-floor penthouse and Hallie on the twenty-ninth floor. They always went to school together.

"Never mind about the clothes," Kendra said, staring at herself in the mirror and still not liking what she saw. "Do I look okay?"

Hallie blew her curly red bangs up off her forehead, crossed her arms, and eyed Kendra's image. Her friend's dark hair and almond-shaped eyes suited the gray sweater and skirt perfectly. And the blue pendant at her neck brought out the blue in her eyes. Hallie frowned and said, "Kendra, you look absolutely, terribly . . . wonderful, as usual."

It was true—Kendra never looked anything other than great, even when her hair was dirty and she wore her sloppiest clothes. "I know people who would kill for those eyes of yours," Hallie added.

When Kendra smiled, it was like a burst of sunlight. She had always been singled out as the prettiest in the class. She didn't think it was such a big deal. She was much more pleased that she studied hard and was a straight-A student.

"What's up? Don't tell me you're dressing up for a calculus test."

"Hallie, how could you forget?" Kendra practically shouted. "Today is the most important day of my life."

Her friend looked puzzled.

"I'm going to be on TV!"

"Oh, that's right," Hallie said. "I totally forgot! Now I understand why you're so crazy. But you look perfect! Just like a real newscaster. Honest."

"I look nervous. And I'm too fat. Did you know that the camera automatically makes you look ten pounds heavier?"

Hallie eyed Kendra's slender waist and said, "Ken, don't be ridiculous." Then she glanced at her watch. "Come on, we're going to be late."

Kendra shoved her books into her leather backpack and the two friends raced down the hall. "And I didn't even get to eat breakfast," she said.

"Wait a sec." Hallie dashed into the kitchen, grabbed a muffin and a banana, and handed them to Kendra. She and Kendra had been friends so long she knew exactly where everything was. "Eat this on the way."

"I'm too nervous to eat."

"Eat!" her friend ordered as they headed for the door. Then she turned to Kendra. "Hey, where's your sister?

"She left already," Kendra said, nibbling on the muffin.

"Just as well," Hallie said. Kendra knew Hallie was a little jealous of the close friendship between the sisters.

"Oh, come on, Lauren never did anything to you," Kendra defended Lauren.

"Well, I could argue that point," Hallie said as they bumped shoulders going out the door.

✦ ✦ ✦

Wilbraham Academy, their exclusive private school on the Upper East Side of Manhattan, was close by. The girls usually walked if the weather wasn't bad. Today, though, they caught the Fifth Avenue bus in front of their building, making it just as the doors of the bus started to close.

They flashed their school passes at the driver. He grunted, closed the doors, and started plowing down the avenue to the next bus stop.

"Great," Kendra muttered, "just what I need, a crowded bus." She tried not to mess her outfit as she and Hallie wriggled through the crush of commuters to find a few spare inches of space where they could stand and breathe at the same time. She was always amazed at the number of people that could squeeze on to a bus. And she marveled at the way everyone managed to keep their balance—the way this guy drove tossed them around like sacks of potatoes. Kendra tried to balance her muffin and banana in one hand, clutch the bus's metal pole in the other, and avoid bumping into the blue-suited man two inches from her face.

Hallie didn't seem to mind the crowd. She shouted above the bus roar to Kendra, "I think it's cool that you're back together with Neil again."

"Well, he's more fun than before and . . ."

"Ouch!" A large lady standing next to them glared at Kendra. "Watch where you swing that thing."

"Sorry," Kendra apologized politely. The bus had swerved, and her backpack had slammed into the woman's shoulder.

"You and Neil are like yo-yos," Hallie said. "You're up, you're down, on-again, off-again. What's the deal, anyway?"

"It's just that I hate when he gets too serious. I need more space."

Just then the bus stopped abruptly. Hallie lost her balance and stepped down hard on the blue-suit's foot.

"Watch it!" he whirled around and glowered at Kendra.

"Sorry," she said, even though she hadn't done it. She didn't feel like arguing right now.

Hallie whispered thanks and then said, "Aren't you worried that he'll take you seriously the next time you drop him?"

"So what? The world won't end or anything. . . ."

"Hey, look out!" a woman with a briefcase shouted.

"Sorry, sorry!" Kendra and Hallie sang out together.

"No, not you," the woman said. "Him." She pointed at a grouchy man next to her. "He almost poked my eye out with his newspaper."

Kendra eyed Hallie, and the two got a fit of giggles that had everyone around them staring, which only made them laugh harder.

Finally, they made it the twelve blocks to Wilbraham Academy. They heard the warning bell ring as they headed toward the large white building. Hallie spotted several kids she knew sitting on the steps. They were all crowded around Judy Matthews, a sort-of friend of Kendra's.

With her long honey-blonde hair and green eyes, Judy was almost as beautiful as Kendra. But the two girls had very different personalities. Judy was lazy about schoolwork, while Kendra took her work very seriously. And Kendra couldn't possibly compete with Judy's skills as an athlete—or a flirt.

Kendra's dark eyes widened when she saw whom Judy was flirting with now. Her very own boyfriend. Tall, good-looking, sandy-haired Neil Jarmon was so caught up in what Judy was saying that he didn't notice Kendra coming up the steps.

"Hey, Neil," she said.

When he saw Kendra, Neil jumped to his feet with unmistakable guilt written on his face. Quickly, he wrapped his arm around Kendra's shoulder, kissed her neck, and said, "I've been looking for you. Are you ready to go on camera this afternoon?"

"As ready as I'll ever be," Kendra replied. But at the thought, she felt a tight knot in her stomach. Great, how could she be a journalist if she panicked whenever she thought about appearing on camera?

"You'll be fine," Hallie said, encouraging her friend.

"You did great in rehearsals," Neil noted. He was in her Communications class, too. But he'd been working in front of the camera for weeks already. "You're not nervous, are you?"

"A little," Kendra admitted. "But as long as Mr. Taylor thinks I can do it, I'm not sweating it."

"That's good," said Judy, who had just risen from the steps. "Because you know," she flicked a strand of her long blonde hair back, "everybody in the whole school will be watching you."

Hallie gave Judy a dirty look, but Kendra just said, "I know." For the first time, though, Kendra wished that Wilbraham Academy wasn't so high-tech. The school had an elaborate closed-circuit TV hookup into each classroom. General news, school news, and special events were broadcast from its studio into each class during the last period every day. Each student in the Communications class had to prepare a news story during the semester. Kendra had been waiting for this day, and she wasn't going to let anything ruin it.

Just then the final bell rang, and everybody ran off to their first period.

Kendra didn't have to try to pay full attention during her first period calculus test. The difficult questions kept her fully occupied. But after that, her mind kept coming back to what was going to happen in front of the camera. For the first time, she found it almost impossible to concentrate. And worse, it seemed like forever until the last period finally arrived.

She made a quick stop in the bathroom to make sure her hair and makeup looked okay. She winked at her image in the mirror and said, "Okay, this is it, and I know you can do it." Then she took a deep breath and headed for the TV studio.

The lights in the control room were low. What lighting there was came from the blinking panels and monitors.

At the controls, Mr. Taylor was instructing one of the students. With barely a glance at Kendra, he held out his hand for the script she had written. It was her first piece, a "soft news" story about the city's efforts to plant and maintain the sidewalk trees on small plots in front of the school. The story would go on a teleprompter so that she could look into the camera and read from the scrolling screen above it at the same time.

Kendra leaned over the shoulder of a classmate at the largest console and peered at the television monitor. On the screen she saw Neil's image. He was seated at the broadcast desk in the studio, warming up in front of the camera.

She watched Neil closely, admiring the ease with which he delivered his story. But he's been doing this for weeks now, she told herself. His voice came through low and steady. And his face did look calm. But then Kendra looked through the soundproof glass into the studio and saw Neil's hands twitching on his notes and his feet shuffling below the desk. The part of him that didn't show on the screen looked as nervous as she felt! She turned back to the monitor.

Without warning, Kendra heard a strange but vaguely familiar sound—the gentle tinkling of crystal chimes. A swirl of firefly lights began to circle Neil's head. Her lips opened in amazement. She couldn't tear her eyes from the screen.

As she watched, Neil's face disappeared. In its place was a man—the most gorgeous young man she had ever seen. His hair was blond, almost golden. His eyes blazed with an electric blue fire that nearly hypnotized her. He smiled at her from the screen.

A wave of dizziness swept over her. She felt her heart beating like a wild thing trying to escape from her body. Her breath came in short gasps. She stared at the vision before her. She was overwhelmed by a feeling she had never known before. Who? . . . The question tried to form in her mind, but she was too thrilled at the sight to care.

Suddenly, for a second, she felt a sharp pain on the back of her hand. She winced, but the face on the monitor commanded her attention. Helplessly, she smiled in wonderment and joy at the screen.

The golden vision nodded and smiled back. His eyes held hers captive.

"Kendra," he whispered softly through the monitor. "The time has come at last. We will soon be together. But you must go home now. Hurry. Hurry home. Your father is waiting for you."

CHAPTER 3

Kendra gasped and bent closer to the monitor.

Mr. Taylor and the student at the controls looked at her in surprise.

Did she just hear what she thought she heard? She blinked and shook her head to clear her mind. The chimes had stopped. On the monitor, Neil's familiar face again vibrated in the electronic light of the screen.

In a flash, she knew that no one else had seen what she had seen. Only she had heard the chimes. Only she had marveled at that soft, compelling voice. But what did it mean? Her father was dead. Who was waiting for her at home? And who was the incredible man on the monitor?

The warning tingle prickled, softly now. Kendra stared at the mark on her hand and rubbed it. It was something she had learned not to ignore. What danger was it warning her of now? She had to get out of the studio, she had to get home—now!

"Are you all right, Kendra?" Mr. Taylor asked.

"You look pale. Do you want to sit down for a minute? There's nothing to be nervous about." He touched her shoulder in concern.

Kendra jumped. "N-no, I have to go. I-I can't . . . not today. I'm sorry."

She turned and ran out of the studio, breathless and terrified.

The bus was too slow, so she hailed a taxi on Madison Avenue for the short ride to her apartment. She was home in record time, panting with fear as she rode the elevator up to the penthouse.

Her hands were so cold and clammy that she fumbled clumsily with her door key. But before she could put the key into the lock, the door was pulled open.

Lauren stood there. She had Study Hall last period and students were sometimes allowed to leave early. Her eyes started to flood when she saw Kendra. Red blotches bloomed on her cheeks as the tears spilled over.

"What happened?" Kendra almost screamed at Lauren.

"Oh, darling, I'm so glad you're home!" Dinah's voice trilled from inside the apartment. "Come here. I have exciting news for you, and I want you to meet someone. Hurry!"

"What's wrong? What is it?" Kendra hissed at Lauren.

Lauren just shook her head as tears trickled down her face.

Kendra put her arm around her sister's shoulders and walked her toward the living room.

Dinah was lounging on the huge white sofa, her legs tucked under her. She looked especially chic in a white silk suit that Kendra hadn't seen before. She was smiling nervously, and her face was flushed. A tall, handsome, gray-haired man sat next to her. When Kendra and Lauren walked into the room, he rose and stood there, smiling at both of them.

"Now, don't be too angry at me, sweetie," Dinah told Kendra. "I know I should have told you first, but it was all so sudden. Wasn't it, darling?" She looked up at the man, then back at Kendra.

Darling?

Lauren twisted out from under her sister's arm and walked to one of the large windows overlooking the park.

Dinah pressed her lips together in annoyance. Then her mood changed. She smiled at her older daughter. "Meet Graham Vanderman, Kendra. He's your new father—well, stepfather. We just got married—at City Hall. It was so romantic! I know you're going to be good friends, so promise me, no scolding."

Graham Vanderman came toward Kendra. His hand was outstretched. "I won't blame you if you're a little angry," he said. "But please don't hold it against me." His warm brown eyes looked deeply into hers. "I've heard so many wonderful things about you—and about Lauren. I've been terribly impatient to meet you. Will you forgive me for whisking your mother away and marrying her?"

It was an oddly formal speech, and Kendra wondered if he had practiced it. But he looked so sincere and friendly that she couldn't help holding out her hand in response. He took it and pressed it between both of his large warm hands.

Kendra opened her mouth but found herself too stunned to say anything. She knew that Dinah dated men, lots of them. After all, she'd been a widow for many years, and she was still a very beautiful woman. But Kendra had had no idea that there was anyone special. Dinah was always so secretive. How like her to sneak off and get married without giving Kendra and Lauren even a hint. No wonder her sister was so upset! And Kendra was angry—but at her mother, not Graham Vanderman.

He released her hand and stepped back to admire her. "You're even prettier than your mother told me, both you and your sister. I do want us to get along, Kendra. It will make me very unhappy if I don't have your approval."

"Uh, well, congratulations, Mr., uh, Vanderman. . . ." Kendra felt like a stammering jerk, but she couldn't think of anything else to say.

"No, no. None of that 'Mr.' I'm Graham—to you and Lauren." He looked toward the window where Lauren was brooding.

Lauren wheeled away from them and ran out of the room.

"Go after her, will you, Kendra?" Dinah said. "She's really making a terrible fuss."

"Let me," Graham said to Dinah. "Please. She's upset with me for intruding on your lives. Let me try to make it better."

Dinah shrugged and watched him follow Lauren out of the living room. Then she patted the sofa next to her. Kendra sat down.

"Isn't he wonderful!" Dinah cried. "I know you're going to be crazy about him. We met in France three months ago, and Graham says it was love at first sight. Imagine, at my age!" She patted her sleek blonde hair. There was no doubt in Kendra's mind that her mother wasn't the least bit surprised that a man would tumble headover-heels in love with her. Kendra knew all about Dinah's power to charm men. Dinah was used to having her way with men, and Kendra knew her mother was too beautiful—and too spoiled—to break the habit. Kendra silently promised herself she'd never become that spoiled.

"You could have warned us," Kendra grumbled. "At least, if we had met him first, or if you had told us there was someone special—we wouldn't have minded so much. This way, I mean, look how shocked Lauren is." Her voice trailed off. She knew Dinah would just slip away from any unpleasant discussion, so there was no use pressing the point.

"Yes, of course, you're right, dear. But she'll get over it. And everything will be perfect. You'll see.

Now, I have more exciting news for you. We're moving!"

"What?"

"That's right—moving. Isn't that wonderful?"

"Where to?" Kendra felt suddenly sick. Did this mean leaving her friends, her school—and the city? It was too awful to think about! "Are we leaving New York?"

"Certainly not! I couldn't breathe any place else. We're just getting out of this tired old apartment—oh, I can't wait!—and you won't believe where we'll be living. . . ."

Moving. "No! We can't!" Kendra looked around the living room. Even if they were staying in New York, she was still horrified to think she'd have to leave the home she had grown up in. She loved every room of their big, sunny apartment. This was where her father had read her those wonderful bedtime stories and helped her with her homework. She'd have to give up her lovely room that she had decorated herself and filled with all her favorite treasures. But even worse was the thought of all the memories she'd be leaving behind. Memories of her father, her childhood, her first real boyfriend. She already felt as if she were losing her identity.

For the first time, Kendra realized that Dinah's marriage would mean more than just accepting a new person into their lives. Lots of things were about to change.

"I don't want to live anywhere but here," Kendra said.

"Well, you didn't think that Graham was going to move in with us, did you?" Dinah said, as if the thought was too ridiculous to mention. As usual, Dinah didn't bother explaining her reasoning. She didn't even bother reasoning. Whenever she thought something should be done a certain way, she expected everyone else to agree. "I wouldn't dream of suggesting it."

"Why not?" Kendra said desperately. "We've got plenty of room here. We've got two extra bedrooms that no one's used in years." One of them had been her father's study. After his death, Dinah had immediately redecorated it into a guest room. The other was used for storage. "You could even knock down a wall and make a really huge bedroom off the terrace on the other side of the apartment and . . ."

Dinah wasn't even listening.

"Graham has a mansion on 76th Street that overlooks the river," Dinah said. "Imagine, a mansion—gardens and acres of land, right in the middle of Manhattan! It's been in his family for generations. I can't wait for you to see it. It's so enormous you can get lost inside. You and Lauren will have a whole floor to yourselves. You're going to love it. I promise."

"I don't want to move," Kendra said. "This is our home."

"You'll feel right at home in Graham's house in a couple of days, darling. We'll all be together, and you and your sister will have lots more space. Wait till you see how Graham fixed up your rooms. You'll both have your own phones. Everything is just perfect!"

Kendra was surprised. "How long have you been planning this?" she asked. "I thought you said you got married on the spur of the moment."

"Well, yes, we did. But of course I told him all about you and Lauren when we first met—do you know, he proposed to me on our second date? When I finally said yes, he decided we should get married right away and live in his house. I guess he wanted you to be comfortable as soon as we moved in, so he went ahead and decorated your rooms and—oh, why are you asking so many questions? Tomorrow you'll see the house. I know you'll love it as much as I do."

"Couldn't Lauren and I stay here?" Kendra asked tentatively, hopelessly. "We're old enough to be on our own, and I'd keep an eye on her. Besides, you wouldn't be far away."

"Don't be silly. Ah, Graham, here you are. I've just been telling Kendra all about your house, and she's thrilled. How is Lauren?"

"She's fine. She's just washing her face. We had a nice talk. We've decided to start by being friends, with an option to get closer later on." He looked at Kendra, mock seriousness on his face.

"How about you, Kendra? Would you like to make the same deal?"

"You're not going to treat me like a child, are you?" Kendra asked. But she couldn't help laughing. He really was nice, and he was trying very hard.

"I wouldn't dream of it. Deal?"

"You bet."

"Good," he said, smiling. "Now that that's settled, we can make plans. Tomorrow I'll take you to see your new home. And you'll meet Anthony."

"Anthony?" Kendra asked. She turned to Dinah. What else had her mother neglected to tell her?

Graham seemed surprised, too. "I'm afraid in all the excitement we forgot to mention my son. Anthony's nineteen. He'll be home from college this evening, and he's looking forward to meeting you at the house tomorrow. We'll all go out for a celebration lunch, if that's okay with you."

It was too much—a new stepfather, a new stepbrother, and a new home in less than an hour.

"Sure," Kendra said dully. "I guess I'll go see how Lauren is."

I won't cry, she thought as she left the room.

✦ ✦ ✦

In bed that night, Kendra tossed fitfully, trying to fall asleep. Just before she dropped off, she remembered the gorgeous man on the TV monitor who had sent her home to meet her "father." Suddenly, the mark on her hand began tingling.

CHAPTER 4

"Where is this place?" Lauren asked Kendra. They left the sidewalk at 76th Street and walked up a curving, tree-shaded path. The noise of construction on the street behind them gradually faded to a dull clanging. They passed through a heavy iron gate with spiked posts and continued up the path. The air was becoming dense and oppressive—and cold.

Beyond the gate, Graham's house emerged bit by bit through the leafy branches. Kendra began to feel a choking sensation, as if something—or someone—had grabbed her throat. Was this their new home? This dark and forbidding place? As the girls came closer, its size alone awed them.

"It's a castle!" Lauren said, laughing.

Kendra stared up at the stone fortress with growing dread. She said nothing.

Graham had told them the house was more than two hundred years old. It was massive, as grand as any they'd ever seen. Its weathered gray stone walls were covered by vines of ivy and greenish moss. Gabled peaks with narrow windows crowned the top. A gloomy porch, dark and foreboding behind columns and arches, stretched across the front of the house. Slanting stone steps led up through the main arch to a heavy wooden front door.

But, old as the house was, it was in perfect condition. Someone had taken great trouble with the grounds, too. Flowering bushes surrounded the house, and manicured lawns spread out on all sides. Off to the left stood a grove of huge and ancient trees. Past the lawn on the right, the girls saw a stone well and a small shingled building with its own garage and garden.

Yet even with its flowers and gardens and grass and trees, the grounds were somber, the house dark and eerie. Everything seemed shrouded in a chilly breeze.

Kendra rubbed her icy hands. She listened for the chatter of city birds, but there were no pigeons murmuring in the grass. Instead of the cheerful chirping of sparrows and the sweet warbling of finches, Kendra heard screeching and cawing. She looked up and noticed hundreds of huge blackbirds lurking in the trees, as if waiting to pounce on some unsuspecting prey.

Kendra shivered.

Why am I so frightened?

Together, the girls moved quietly up the path.

"Dracula must have lived here before Graham's family moved in," Lauren whispered.

Again Kendra was silent. She didn't feel like joking. A force inside the house was pulling her forward, and she felt overwhelmed. Something menacing lurked behind that heavy wooden door. The very walls seemed to shriek "Danger." Something terrifying—but oddly thrilling—waited for her inside. Kendra walked forward, drawn by invisible strings, as if someone else were controlling her movements.

"Oh, look!" Lauren cried, pointing. "You can see the river down there." It was a sight familiar to the girls from the high terrace of their apartment, but it had been a long time since they had seen the Hudson so close. They could even make out the faces of the crews of ships and tugs gliding through the currents. "Come on, Kennie! Wave!"

Kendra didn't respond. She was looking up at a window on the third floor. Someone had pushed aside a curtain and was staring down at them. As Kendra looked, the curtain fluttered, and the face was gone.

"Earth to Kendra," Lauren said. "Hello there. Where'd you go? You look like a zombie."

Suddenly, with throaty barking, a large black Labrador retriever bounded out of the trees and rushed at the girls.

"Max! Come back here," a male voice called. "Hey, Max, behave yourself!"

But Max had his own idea of good behavior. He rushed up to the girls, barking wildly. His heavy tail thumped on Lauren's leg. She laughed with delight.

A tall, good-looking guy followed Max out of the woods. "Oh, Max, you have no class," he scolded, pulling the dog's collar. "Hi. I'm Anthony Vanderman. And you're Kendra and Lauren—or Lauren and Kendra, if I got you backwards. I'm glad to meet you, and Max apologizes for losing his cool."

Speaking of cool, Kendra thought. Anthony was really good-looking and very sure of himself. She sensed him studying her, sizing her up.

The girls introduced themselves, Lauren hugging and patting the ecstatic Max. Lauren loved all animals, a feeling that was usually mutual.

"Come on inside. I'll show you around," Anthony said. "Dinah and Graham should be back soon. Then I guess we're all going out for lunch."

With Max panting happily at her side, Lauren followed Anthony up the steps, onto the dark terrace, up to the massive front door.

Kendra lingered a moment longer. Behind her, on the street, she could still hear the noise of a construction project. The workmen raising the scaffolding shouted to each other. The cranes and girders and heavy equipment clanged away insistently.

When she and Lauren had passed the site on

their way to the path, they had seen workmen in hard hats crawling over the rising structure. It was almost half built now. Graham had warned the girls that a new high-rise apartment was going up in front of his property. He seemed pleased, though Kendra couldn't understand why. She thought the construction mess was ugly. Up close, the noise was deafening. The new building would cast shadows and make the grounds even darker.

When Kendra asked Graham why he didn't mind, he explained that he looked forward to more privacy. The new building would completely hide his house from the street. He'd grown tired of curious people staring at the mansion. Some even came up the front path to get a closer look. Kendra didn't blame them. The house was amazing, even if it was a bit creepy.

A curtain fluttered in one of the windows upstairs again, this time on the second floor. Was someone coming down to greet them?

Kendra hurried up the steps and followed her sister through the door.

✦ ✦ ✦

"Welcome to our humble home," Anthony said. His voice echoed through the marble entrance hall, a foyer larger than the living room of the girls' apartment. An elaborate curved staircase rose to the second floor, dominating the hall. Anthony waited politely while the girls gazed around in wonder. It was an impressive sight. Then Anthony said lightly, "I'll give you the short tour now and let Graham give you the full treatment later."

Before they could move, Kendra heard the sharp click of hard heels coming through a doorway on the right. A thin woman in a dark gray dress entered the hall. Her hands were pressed together, and her unsmiling face was turned to Anthony as if she hadn't noticed Kendra and Lauren.

"Hi, Mrs. Stavros." Anthony looked suddenly uncomfortable. "Look, here they are at last. Meet Kendra and Lauren Linton." He turned to the girls. "Mrs. Stavros is our housekeeper. She runs this place, and I think she runs us, too."

"Hi," Lauren said, holding out her hand to the housekeeper.

Mrs. Stavros took it without much enthusiasm and let it drop quickly. "I'm pleased to meet you." Her glance moved from Lauren to Kendra. "I hope you'll be comfortable here. If I can do anything for you, please let me know."

"Thank you," Kendra said, not offering her own hand. "I think I saw you in the upstairs window as I was coming up the path."

"You couldn't have. I've been back in the kitchen most of the morning. Max! Out!" Mrs. Stavros spoke sharply to the big black Lab, who was cowering behind Anthony. Max's nails scratched on the marble floor as he slunk reluctantly out the front door. She watched him go. Then she returned her attention to the girls. "When do you think you'll be moving in? I'll want to have everything ready for you and your mother."

Kendra hesitated. "I really don't know."

Mrs. Stavros stared hard at Kendra. Kendra shivered inwardly. "Well, if you don't need me right now, I'll get back to my work."

They watched her return to the back of the house. "She's not super-friendly," Anthony said. "But she's been with us forever, and we couldn't manage without her. You'll get used to her."

"Yeah, sure," Kendra mumbled.

For the next half hour, Anthony showed them around the main floor of the house.

The girls marveled at the many vast, shadowy rooms. They admired the old paintings of the Vanderman family, the elegant antiques and furniture. Sometimes they stopped to study a particular piece as if they were in a museum. Lauren was especially impressed with the huge chest that contained Graham's weapons collection. It only made Kendra shiver. She hated guns and wondered why someone as gentle and nice as Graham would be so fascinated with them.

"Now comes the spooky part." Anthony was smiling as he opened a hidden door in the front hall.

The girls found themselves groping their way through a network of dark, twisting corridors. Lauren gripped Kendra's hand in sudden fear. The corridors seemed to wind around in circles. Some descended to a dank basement below. A cold, mildewy draft rose to chill their bones. Kendra knew that one wrong turn would leave her hopelessly lost. "The house was a stop on the Underground Railroad in the 1800s," Anthony explained. His voice echoed along the passageway. "The corridors were constructed with dead ends and hidden doors. They were a safe place for runaway slaves to hide when they were being chased."

"That's so cool," Lauren said.

"It's a little creepy," Kendra said. The maze made her uncomfortable—even if it was built for a good cause. She suspected that Anthony was enjoying her discomfort.

Finally, Anthony led them out of the maze and back into the main hall. The girls sighed with relief when he closed the door to the corridors behind them. Graham and Dinah had just arrived. It was late, so they all bustled to leave for the celebration lunch that Graham had planned. The rest of the tour would have to wait.

At the front door, something made Kendra look back.

The tinkling chimes. They were calling to her again.

She looked up the staircase. Smiling down at her from the top step was the beautiful golden-haired man from her vision. Lights danced around his head. Even though he was at the top of the stairs, his voice sounded very close—whispering in her ear, "I've waited so long for you, Kendra. Now you've come. You're home at last. And we'll never be separated again."

Startled, Kendra ran to catch up with the others. She didn't notice the tingling sensation on the back of her hand.

"Who was that man in the house?" Kendra asked Graham as she joined him on the path to the street. Dinah, Lauren, and Anthony were ahead of them. Lauren and Anthony were jabbering away like old friends.

"You must mean Mr. Stavros," Graham said. "Anthony tells me you've already met his wife, our housekeeper."

"That's her husband?" Kendra said.

"He works here, too." Graham took Kendra's arm to guide her past the construction mess on the sidewalk. "He looks after the gardens and grounds. Whatever needs doing, Mr. Stavros is the one to call. You'll meet him later. He's really very nice, even if he does look like an ogre with all that thick black hair and bushy mustache."

"No, I meant the blond man I saw at the top of the stairs."

Graham stopped and looked at her for a moment. "You must be mistaken. There's no one else in the house. Let's catch up with the others, shall we?"

I'm not mistaken, Kendra thought. I know what I saw—I know what I heard.

CHAPTER 5

Kendra looked around the apartment. She felt a terrible pain sear her heart. Tomorrow she would leave her home forever. Kendra had to move into that huge brooding place that terrified her in a way she didn't understand. But, somehow, it also excited her. Kendra thought it was weird that the house could frighten and attract her at the same time!

Still, how could Dinah believe it would ever feel as welcoming as their own apartment? This was her real home, and she would never see it again. The thought was unbearable!

As much as she loved it, Kendra had to admit that the apartment was a mess now. Carpets had been pulled up, leaving gritty floors that crunched underfoot. The drapes and curtains were gone, so the light that filtered through the remaining window blinds was stark and harsh. No more paintings on the walls, no more books on the shelves. Most of the furniture was still there, but everything looked different now—so cold and sterile.

Especially since the apartment did not belong to them anymore.

Dinah had given the furniture away to several charities. "I want a fresh beginning," she said. The movers did all the work, of course. Dinah just pointed to things and said "Out" or "Move." Kendra had wanted to keep the old pipe rack that had belonged to her father, but Dinah insisted that the movers put it in one of the charity boxes. The volunteers from the charities would collect everything the following week. The rooms looked so—sad.

Our last night home.

Stacks of packing cartons were piled in every room. It was impossible to walk in a straight line from one place to another. Huge cartons filled with their clothing and personal belongings stood in the hall. Dinah's treasures—crystal, china, silver—had already been moved to Graham's house. It was hard for Kendra to care about material things when many of her fondest memories were being left behind, held forever in the apartment's walls.

Kendra wandered through the silent rooms, trying to fight her depression. This had been her home all her life and now it felt alien to her. How would she feel tomorrow?

She stepped out onto the wide section of terrace that faced east, toward the river. The sun was setting behind her, and stripes of fiery red flashed in the water.

She looked down toward 76th Street. From here, she could see the construction site and the beginnings of the gigantic new high-rise apartment building. Beyond it, she could see the green acres of Graham's yard and the light gray stones of his house. Funny, she had never noticed the house before. From the height of her terrace it looked like a doll's house. Graham's grand ancestral mansion. Her new home.

She shuddered with sudden cold.

Graham had been so nice to them all. Why did she keep thinking there was something strange about him? She had no explanation for her uneasiness—only a feeling of discomfort. She couldn't shake the sense that he was hiding something.

"Oh, Kennie, there you are!" Lauren rushed out onto the terrace. Her face was flushed, and she looked upset. "Have you seen Grimbal? I've looked all over, and he's missing. I can't go without him!" she moaned.

Kendra smiled. Grimbal was Lauren's ancient, battered teddy bear. He had been bigger than Lauren when their father brought him home. He remained her lifelong security object. Kendra could remember her sister as a child gravely repeating their father's bedtime stories to Grimbal. Lauren would get them scrambled and backwards, but they still sounded wonderful. Kendra didn't admit it then, but she loved listening to Lauren's upside-down tales.

"Remember?" Kendra said. "Dinah made you pack him in a carton the other day. She didn't think it would be cool for you to arrive at Graham's with a battered stuffed animal in your arms."

"Oh, of course! I forgot." Lauren made a face. "I guess he is kind of babyish."

"That's okay," Kendra said. "He was your first love, after all."

Lauren crossed the terrace and stood next to Kendra. She threw her arm around her sister's shoulders and squeezed.

"I'm so excited! I can't wait for tomorrow! How about you?"

"Won't you miss it here?" Kendra asked.

"Sure I will, but it's going to be so terrific in Graham's house. All that room! We could sleep in a different bedroom every night if we wanted to!"

"It isn't exactly cramped here, you know. And the view is something else—"

"Hey!" Lauren's arm shot out over the terrace railing, pointing. "There's the house! Oh, cool! I bet if we hadn't packed the binoculars we could see Anthony or Graham in the gardens."

"You really like Graham, don't you?"

Lauren nodded. "I almost hate to admit it, but I do. I mean he makes me feel special. Like, he'd do anything to make me happy. Aren't you glad Dinah married him?"

Kendra hesitated. Was she glad about Graham?

Was she happy about becoming part of his family?

A sudden vision of the golden-haired man at the top of Graham's stairs crossed Kendra's mind. Who was he? And how come Graham didn't seem to know what she was talking about when she asked about him?

Kendra had never held back her feelings from Lauren before. What was making her so reluctant to share them now? Kendra realized that Lauren was waiting for her to answer.

"Yeah, I'm glad," she told Lauren. For Dinah maybe . . . but am I glad for me? she wondered.

Standing there on the apartment terrace, looking down at Graham's house, Kendra felt mostly fear. But, also, a strange sense of excitement. She was eager—but about what? Until now, tomorrow's move had filled her with dread. Now part of her was actually looking forward to it. Was it because of her golden man?

Will I see him again? Kendra was aware of a sudden longing. Why did the thought of the golden man thrill her so?

I want to see him. I want him to come closer so I can really look at him.

But would he bring joy or sorrow into her life?

She shivered, although the early evening air was not cold.

"What's wrong, Kennie?" Lauren was staring at her, concern wrinkling her forehead. "Are you so quiet because tonight's our last night here?"

"I guess."

"I think something else is bothering you," Lauren said. "Is it something bad? Tell me. You've been acting so weird lately—ever since we met Graham. Something is wrong, isn't it? You look so sad all of a sudden—and scared."

"No, I'm not scared. I'm just sorry to be leaving here." Kendra pulled Lauren's long blonde pony-tail and gave her sister a quick hug. "Nothing's wrong. Stop worrying about me. You'll see. Everything's going to be fine."

Will it? Will it really?

She turned away so Lauren couldn't see the confusion and uneasiness on her face.

"Oh, girls! For heaven's sake!" Dinah appeared at the door of the terrace. "Are you two just standing around moping? Graham will be here any minute, and you're not dressed for dinner. I told you, he's taking us to a very special restaurant tonight. I expect you to look your best. Please go change your clothes—I hope you've still got something decent here to wear—and please change those gloomy expressions on your faces, too."

She shooed them off the terrace and back to their rooms.

Lauren nudged Kendra as they separated at the doors to their rooms. "Look on the bright side," she said. "From tomorrow on, Dinah will be living on a different floor."

Kendra laughed. "Here's to tomorrow!"

✦ ✦ ✦

Kendra hadn't realized how sleepy she was. She was yawning when Graham and Anthony dropped them off at their apartment after dinner.

As soon as she got upstairs, she trudged into the bathroom where her remaining cosmetics waited to be packed in the morning. She checked her medicine cabinet. Almost empty. It used to be so colorful, crammed with makeup and creams and brushes. Now it looked so sad. She picked up her toothbrush and scrubbed mechanically. Face washed and hair brushed, she couldn't wait to get to bed. Kendra closed the medicine-cabinet door and stared into its mirror.

She couldn't see her face.

Lights danced in the glass, almost blinding her. The music of the crystal chimes rang in her ears.

Her golden man. He was there—in the mirror—smiling out at her!

"Tomorrow you will come to me, Kendra. We will be together at last. You will be mine. Tomorrow!"

The man's image faded suddenly as searing pain gripped the mark on Kendra's hand.

CHAPTER 6

Kendra was glad to relax and try to get used to their new home on 76th Street after the excitement of moving.

Anthony hovered around Kendra and Lauren, offering to help. But there was nothing useful that he could do, so he was really in the way. Finally, Kendra had told him—politely—that they didn't need any help. Max had sneaked past Mrs. Stavros and crept upstairs to the third floor. He wagged his tail in encouragement as he bounced between Kendra's and Lauren's rooms. They noticed he didn't bark. That would have alerted the housekeeper, and Mrs. Stavros had already made it clear that she didn't like him in the house. Between Anthony, Max, and making sure that everything was put away in the right drawers, Kendra was wiped out.

Alone now, she sat at the edge of her bed and yawned. Almost everything was sorted out and put away. She looked around her new room. It was so pretty, so personal and cozy—so familiar.

She was puzzled.

A sudden, sick feeling churned in the pit of her stomach.

It just wasn't right.

How had Graham created a room almost identical to the one she had decorated herself in the apartment on Fifth Avenue? There was the twin of Kendra's great canopied bed, with fluffy pink covers to match the skirt that draped her dressing table. The lights surrounding her makeup mirror . . . the pink and gray carpet . . . the lamps with their soft rosy shades . . . the white wood desk—everything was exactly the same.

Of course, Dinah might have told Graham or even shown the rooms to him. Still, it was eerie. It was all so intimate, so personal. Instead of feeling grateful, Kendra felt as though her privacy had been invaded. How had Graham known so much about her taste? Dinah must have helped but, Kendra thought, Dinah never paid much attention to Kendra's possessions as long as she kept them neat.

Obviously, Graham wanted her to be comfortable. He had beamed with pride when he showed her the room. Kendra was touched that he had tried so hard. So why was she so miserable? She hadn't felt this alone and vulnerable since her father died.

She felt a sharp pain on the back of her hand. Her fingers were clenched, and her nails were pressing into her palms. She rubbed her hands and stood up.

Knock it off! Nothing's wrong!

Lauren burst in from her room across the hall.

"Hey, what do you think, Kennie? It's just like home, isn't it? Only bigger and better! How did Graham know?" She was bubbling with excitement as she told Kendra about all the familiar, favorite things that filled her new room. "And guess what, the wallpaper has Arabians just like Vinnie!" Lauren's horse was her pride. She was obviously thrilled that Graham had decorated her room with pictures of sleek Arabians. "Come see!" she insisted.

Lauren dragged Kendra across the hall for an inspection. She couldn't stop chattering as she pointed out every small detail. "Isn't it wonderful!"

No, it's weird.

Kendra wondered how she could point this out to Lauren without worrying her. "Uh, my room's the same. Just like it was in our apartment. It's odd—isn't it? Do you think Dinah took Graham to our old rooms—or showed him pictures?"

"Who cares? Graham is so terrific! I'm going to give him a huge hug when I see him! Look at this! I've got my own phone, too, just like you. And look at my desk. . . ."

Kendra let Lauren rattle on without saying anything else. She didn't want to dampen her sister's enthusiasm. Lauren was happy, and that made

Kendra feel better. She'd never do anything to upset or hurt Lauren. But she realized that, more and more, she was holding back. She couldn't talk about her uneasiness about Graham and Dinah's sudden marriage, or the unexpected duplicates of their rooms. . . .

Or him.

Suddenly, she remembered the golden man. No, she certainly couldn't tell Lauren about the thrilling, terrifying golden man who had invaded her life and her dreams.

It hurt her to know that she wasn't being completely honest with Lauren. Without her sister to confide in, Kendra was utterly alone.

✦ ✦ ✦

Kendra wandered downstairs to the living room. She couldn't help noticing that it was twice as big as the living room in their old apartment. Dinah was busy arranging purple and white tulips in a crystal vase. Her silvery blonde hair was beautifully styled, her makeup was perfect, and she wore a cream-colored dress with long sleeves that fluttered as her hands fussed with the flowers. She looked as glamorous as an actress from an old-fashioned movie.

Unreal, Kendra thought.

Dinah plucked a droopy leaf from a flower as she gave instructions to Mrs. Stavros without even looking at her. The housekeeper's lips were pinched with irritation.

"I'll be inviting more than a hundred people," Dinah was saying. "I want everything to be perfect. You'll have to spruce up all the rooms on this floor. And open the ones in back—how long have they been closed off? Be sure you scrub everything till it shines, shines, shines."

No wonder Mrs. Stavros looked so angry, Kendra thought. As if the whole house wasn't already sparkling clean. In the few days since they had moved in, Kendra had gotten used to seeing the housekeeper bustling through the house from morning to night. From the top floors down to the kitchen in back of the main floor, Mrs. Stavros would pop up unexpectedly, her arms filled with clean laundry or fresh groceries that had just been delivered. At first, Kendra found it spooky. Mrs. Stavros was so quiet that Kendra never knew when or where she would appear. But it was clear that everything ran like clockwork because of the housekeeper. Dinah never could have managed without her. Kendra knew Dinah didn't mean to sound so abrupt when she spoke to Mrs. Stavros, but she almost sounded rude. As much as Kendra loved her mother, she often wished Dinah were more considerate and less self-centered.

"Finish these up," Dinah said to Mrs. Stavros as she abandoned the flowers and took Kendra's hand. "Come into the study with me, darling. I want to tell you all about my plans. It's too exciting! We're going to have a big—no—a huge party. I want to introduce Graham to all our friends!"

Kendra slouched on the big leather sofa next to her mother. After the first gushing sentences, she simply stopped listening.

"You haven't heard a word I've said," Dinah finally complained. "Aren't you interested? I told you that you can invite your own friends, too. I thought you'd be excited." Dinah looked more closely at her daughter. "What's the matter? You're so quiet. Are you coming down with something? This is no time to get sick. Do you have a fever?" She reached out to feel Kendra's forehead, concern at last replacing her annoyance.

Kendra assured Dinah that she was all right. "I just want to ask you something that's been bothering me. How did Graham know how to decorate our rooms? Mine and Lauren's, I mean. They look just like home."

"I suppose I told him. Maybe I showed him the snapshots you and Lauren took of each other when you got that new camera. Really, I can't remember. I know he never came to the apartment until after we were married. Why do you ask? What's wrong with your room? Don't you like it? Your sister seems pleased with hers."

"It's fine. Only, it's . . . well, so similar. It's strange, that's all."

Dinah sighed theatrically. "I don't understand you. When you ought to be happy, you're grouchy. When you should be grateful, you criticize. Graham went to a lot of trouble to make you comfortable, and all you can do is complain. Really, Kendra!"

"I'm not complaining, honestly! I'm just confused. It seems so odd."

"You're too emotional, darling. Your imagination always gets the better of you. There's nothing odd about what Graham did. He wants us to be happy here, all of us. We're his new family. I want you to be very kind to him. What happened a year ago—such a tragedy, you know!"

"No, I don't know. You haven't told us very much about him. What happened?"

"Oh, poor Graham," Dinah said, shaking her head. "His wife —his first wife, Helen—was killed in a terrible accident. It was such a shock. Of course, Graham is still grieving. Anthony, too, even if he doesn't show it. One terrible moment, and the whole family was destroyed. It makes me shudder to think of it. Not that we haven't had our own tragedy, but this . . ."

"What happened?" Kendra prodded her mother.

"Plane crash. They were flying in Graham's private plane, and it just exploded into the side of a mountain. Both of them were killed instantly. Graham had to identify their bodies and the pilot's, too."

"Both of them?"

"His daughter, Syrie. She died with her mother, poor little thing. Such a beautiful child—well, not really a child. They're both buried in the old family cemetery past the gardens. Actually, I find that rather primitive, don't you? A cemetery on your own grounds!" As usual, Dinah took off on a detour, following whatever thought popped into her head. "Still, they couldn't be in a more beautiful place, Helen and Syrie—if it matters to them. Oh, it's too sad! I don't want to think about it anymore!"

Kendra was stunned. Not just by the violent deaths of Graham's first wife and his daughter, but because the name Syrie sounded familiar. Kendra wondered if she had heard it somewhere before.

Dinah stood up. "You will be nice to Graham, won't you? He's suffered terribly."

Kendra started to reassure her, but Dinah's attention had already turned to something else. Without another word, Dinah was on her way to the back of the main floor where she would undoubtedly irritate Mrs. Stavros even more.

Kendra thought some fresh air would do her some good after her talk with Dinah. She stepped out onto the front porch and looked around at the lush green gardens. Beyond them, she could see the big trees that bordered the Vanderman family cemetery.

A fleeting motion caught her eye. A figure was moving in the cemetery. Was it Anthony or Graham visiting the graves? She wouldn't want to disturb them.

"Kendra! Kendra!" Someone was whispering

her name. Someone pleading urgently. Was it the person in the cemetery?

She stared and blinked—and the figure disappeared.

"Kendra!" The voice floated on the air, even more urgent.

Who was calling her?

Suddenly, a force outside herself compelled her. Without knowing why, Kendra felt she had to answer the pleading voice. She must go to whoever was calling her. She felt helpless to resist the eerie power that drew her forward.

Slowly, she walked down the steps and into the garden. She headed toward the cemetery.

"Kendra . . . !"

"Yes, I'm coming." Who is calling me?

She couldn't explain why the name suddenly popped into her thoughts.

"Syrie?" she whispered.

CHAPTER 7

"Kendra!" Anthony waved from the front terrace. Lauren was at his side, also calling to her.

Kendra was halfway to the cemetery when she heard them. She hesitated, turned and walked back to the house.

"What's up?"

"We're going down to The Record Hunter," Lauren said. "Want to come?"

"No, thanks, I'll pass. You go ahead, but be back in time for dinner."

Lauren grinned. "Yeah, yeah, I will. What did I tell you, Anthony? Kendra loves to act like she's my mother."

"Someone has to. See you guys later." Kendra smiled and yanked Lauren's long blonde hair as her sister slipped past and headed down the front steps.

Anthony lingered for a moment. "Where were you heading?"

"I was going to explore the garden," Kendra said. For some reason she didn't understand, she couldn't tell Anthony she was really going to the cemetery. "It's so beautiful here. I promise I won't trample the crocuses, or whatever they are."

"Are you sure you don't want to come with us?"

"Definitely, positively, absolutely sure. You two have a good time. And, Anthony, thanks for being so nice to Lauren."

"I'm just your basic good guy." Anthony shrugged and smiled. He followed Lauren down the steps.

Kendra watched them walk down the path together.

As she entered the house, her memory blurred. Why was I going to the cemetery, anyhow? she wondered.

✦ ✦ ✦

The old house seemed to be breathing.

Kendra woke at midnight with a gasp. The house was creaking and settling, making noises as if it were a huge monster inhaling and exhaling rhythmically.

Inhale, exhale . . . inhale, exhale . . . the breathing seemed to grow louder and louder.

Fear seized Kendra as if she were a child alone at home in the dark. Her throat tightened and her heart beat wildly. She couldn't control her terror.

Kendra squinted as her eyes tried to focus on some glimmer of light. But the room was pitch-black, and the darkness seemed to press on her until she felt she would suffocate.

She was thirsty—desperately thirsty. She sat up in bed. Dim outlines of the furniture emerged from the black. Kendra licked her lips. How she would love a glass of cold juice! She thought of the icy pitcher of orange juice in the refrigerator down in the kitchen. But no, nothing would make her leave her room and go down those dark stairs alone. She pulled the covers around her and rolled over. Her long dark hair fell in tangles over her face.

So thirsty!

Suddenly, she heard the gentle tinkling of chimes.

The sound was the sweetest she had ever heard. It was a sound she had heard before. She was so groggy, she had to struggle to remember. Where—and when?

Of course!

She had heard the song of the chimes often before. The other day, at the top of the stairs. And before that, too. On her last night in their old apartment. And in her dreams. The crystal melody of the chimes began to break through to wake her memory.

She lifted her head.

Fireflies of light danced in the corner across her room. Softly, slowly they took shape. The golden man rose gracefully from the lights and smiled at her.

His voice, sweet as the chimes, wafted across the room.

"At last you have come to me, Kendra!"

CHAPTER 8

She opened her mouth to scream. But she couldn't. Despite her fear, she was thrilled. He was so beautiful, his smile so inviting, that Kendra felt her own smile welcoming him. This was the man she had seen at the top of the stairs . . . and before that, when she thought she was dreaming.

I'm dreaming now. I must be!

She was dazzled as she looked into his flashing eyes.

Who is he? What does he want?

He read her thoughts. "I want us to be together. And you want that, too, don't you? Come to me." The golden vision held out his arms.

Kendra was helpless to resist.

Almost without realizing it, she rose from her bed and walked toward him, her feet barely touching the carpet. Still smiling, she drifted closer to him. He wrapped his powerful arms around her. He was strong and muscular, like an athlete, but he held her gently. Now that she was closer she could see that he was not as old as she'd thought, though he wasn't exactly young, either. There was something ageless about him.

She looked up into his eyes. They were hypnotic, dancing with flecks of gold. He was so handsome.

"Kendra," he whispered. He leaned forward, and his lips brushed hers. His arms tightened around her, and she could feel the electricity between them. He kissed her again. Kendra felt herself growing weak.

I've never been so happy.

Again, he heard her thoughts.

"I will make you even happier," he said. He released her and stepped back, studying her.

Kendra's disappointment struck her like a blow. She didn't want to leave those strong arms. She could still feel his kiss, and she longed to have his lips on hers again. Her hand, under its own spell, rose and reached out to him. He took it and pressed his mouth to the rosy mark on the back. It began to tingle. She rubbed her hand without thinking, out of habit.

The golden man laughed softly. "I put that mark on your hand—to protect you, to save you for the day we could be together," he told her. "Do you remember?"

Kendra shook her head. She couldn't remember anything but his touch. At that moment, she had forgotten the sign that had always warned her of danger in the past.

"Never mind. I'll teach you everything you need to know," he said. "First, you must do what I tell you. Concentrate. That's good. Now, think of the moment just before you saw me. What did you want most then? Remember what you wished for?"

As if hypnotized, Kendra thought of her terrible thirst just before the vision appeared.

There was a soft clinking next to her bed. A tray had materialized on her night table with a frosty pitcher of juice.

"Did you do that?" she asked, stunned.

"No, you did. Drink, Kendra. Then I'll tell you a secret. Our secret."

The juice was deliciously cold. Kendra drank, staring wide-eyed at her visitor over the rim of her glass.

He began to speak in a low voice. It was almost like a chant.

"You are special, Kendra. You are a Sensitive. You were born at the last stroke of midnight, and you have great powers. There are many Sensitives born at midnight, thousands all around the world, but you are exceptional. Your powers are extraordinary. I've come to teach you about them. Soon you'll be able to see and do things you can't even dream of now."

Again, Kendra shook her head. "I've dreamt you, haven't I? You're not real. You're a dream I'm caught in. I'll wake up soon."

"Remember the touch of my hand, my kiss? You know I'm real. I'm here to love you—and to show you how to use your great gifts. I've chosen you especially."

"Why?"

"You're one of the strongest, Kendra. I want you to be strong. Your power will give me eternal life. Then we can be together always."

"I don't have any powers," Kendra protested. "The juice—it was some kind of trick. I didn't do that."

The man shook his head. "Yes, you did. And tomorrow you'll see more of your power. Listen to what I say: Tomorrow, someone who cares about you will dance with death, and someone you care about will be lost."

The twinkling lights began to gather around him. The golden vision was starting to disappear.

"Wait!" Kendra cried. "Don't go. Don't leave me. Tell me who you are."

The soft voice was almost a whisper as it faded away.

"I am yours—and you are mine."

CHAPTER 9

The morning light shimmered through the window curtains. Kendra woke, feeling lightheaded and dizzy. The bedcovers were twisted, hanging half on the floor.

I've had another dream, she thought. But the touch of the golden man lingered, the feel of his lips, his strong arms, his soft voice . . .

She sat up, confused.

There on her night table was the tray with the pitcher!

You idiot! You went down for it yourself last night.

Kendra raced through her shower, then carefully put on her makeup and combed out her long, wavy hair. When she came out of the bathroom to dress, the tray was gone.

Graham and Anthony were already at the table in the sunny breakfast room when Kendra came downstairs. She greeted them cheerfully and remembered their early-morning personalities.

Graham was pleasant and friendly; Anthony was a total grump. Lauren joined them soon. Dinah was having her breakfast—strong black coffee and a stingy half-slice of toast—in her room. Mrs. Stavros carried it up to her with an irritated expression.

"Did you hear anything last night?" Kendra casually asked her sister.

"You bet I did," Lauren said. "This house has more squeaks than my old ten-speed. Say, Graham, you want me to loan you my oil-can?"

He laughed and watched her pile the pancakes on her plate. Lauren was as slender as her older sister, but she ate like her horse, Vinnie. Clearly, Graham approved.

"It's a very old house, Lauren, and its poor, old, tired joints creak, just like mine. Do you think your oil-can will help me, too?"

"You don't complain. Your house does. It doesn't only squeak, it groans and whispers and croaks. Maybe it's haunted," Lauren said hopefully.

"I've heard stories, but no one has ever caught a ghost in the halls. Sorry to disappoint you," Graham said lightly. "Maybe you'd like to invite one to move in. We've got plenty of room."

Anthony looked up from his coffee and laughed at the feeble joke with a short bark. Kendra thought she saw a sly look pass from him to his father. He finished his coffee quickly and left the table with a grunt that could have meant

"Good-bye" or "Have a nice day" or "The house is on fire." Kendra decided that Anthony didn't turn on the charm until later in the day.

Lauren and Kendra stood up and started to leave. As Kendra was following her sister out the door, Graham called to her.

"Do you have a minute, Kendra?"

"Sure." She returned to the table.

"Have another cup of coffee with me. I want to give you something." Graham caught Mrs. Stavros's eye as she passed through the room on her way to the kitchen and asked her to bring them a fresh pot. Then he reached into his pocket and pulled out a small box. He passed it across the table to Kendra with a slightly embarrassed smile. "It's for you. Just a small gift to tell you how happy I am that you've become part of my family. You've brought sunshine back into this old house, you and Lauren. I have something for her, too, but this is especially for you. I hope you like it. Go ahead, open it."

He watched closely as Kendra peeled away the tissue nestled inside the box and pulled out a delicate, old-fashioned bracelet. It was gold and set with blood-red garnets.

"It's beautiful!" Kendra exclaimed. "Oh, Graham, thank you!" She put the bracelet on, marveling at its satin-smooth gold and the fiery red light of its gems. "I love it!"

"I'm so glad," Graham said. He rose and walked around the table. "I have some calls to make, so

I'll leave you for now. We'll see each other at dinner. Enjoy your day."

"I will, especially now. Thanks for the wonderful surprise."

"Thank you, my dear." As he passed her, Graham leaned over and lightly kissed her cheek.

Kendra pushed back the long sleeve of her white blouse and held her hand higher to the sunlight so she could admire the sparkle of the bracelet. It was probably too expensive and she knew she shouldn't, but she had to wear it to school. Kendra couldn't wait to show it to Hallie and her other friends.

Mrs. Stavros entered from the kitchen with a pot of fresh, hot coffee. She looked at the bracelet on Kendra's wrist.

"Oh!" she gasped. Her hand trembled. The pot she was holding shook, and a burst of boiling hot coffee splashed onto Kendra's arm.

"Ow!" Kendra cried out in sudden pain as the coffee scalded her.

Mrs. Stavros set the pot down, apologizing. She was shaking, and her normally pale face was bright red. But Kendra barely noticed. There was an angry red welt on her arm where the coffee had landed, and her white blouse was ruined forever. She jumped up and ran upstairs to put something on her burn and change her blouse. Now she'd be late for school.

Rummaging through a drawer for something

else to wear, she noticed a framed photograph on her desk that hadn't been there before.

What's this? How'd this get here?

She leaned over and studied the photograph. It showed Graham and a pretty woman; both were smiling. Standing between them was an exquisite, serious-looking young girl. The photo had been taken outside in the gardens. Kendra recognized the flower beds and a corner of the front porch of the house. Was that Helen with Graham, and their daughter, Syrie?

Who put the photo there? Kendra wondered. She picked it up to study it closer. A shiver washed over her entire body.

On the girl's slim wrist was the same bracelet Graham had just given her.

✦ ✦ ✦

Kendra absently rubbed the tingling mark on her hand. Warning. Something awful was going to happen today. She was sure of it. All morning a sense of dread hung over her like a dark cloud.

Through all her classes, she was uneasy and restless. When Neil asked if she wanted to have lunch with him, she told him she wasn't going to bother eating. But when noon came, so did her appetite. To her surprise, she was very hungry.

She couldn't find Neil, so she rounded up Hallie and they walked around the corner to the nearby coffee shop that was a hangout for most of the kids at school.

"I'm definitely dieting today," Hallie said. "Nothing but yogurt, green salad, and a Diet Pepsi. What do you think of our French assignment? Write a book report on a contemporary French novel in French! I mean, help!" She paused for air, then rattled on. "Maybe I'll let my hair grow long like yours. Maybe I'll see if I can get my freckles tattooed off. I wonder if they can do that."

One of the nice things about really good friends, Kendra decided, was that you didn't have to pay attention to everything they said. Hallie was always so comfortable to be with.

They entered the Mad Deli on Madison Avenue, and Kendra was glad that they had beaten the crowd. Only a few tables were taken. Hallie headed for one near the back, but Kendra stopped her.

"Not there, please!"

"Oh-oh." Hallie saw the problem right away. A noisy group of guys from Wilbraham was settling into a booth in the back. In their midst was Rob Prentis, class clown, all-around creep, and a pest who couldn't keep his crush on Kendra to himself. He was always obnoxious when she was around. There were no limits to what he'd do to get her attention. Last week, he had embarrassed her in English Composition class by reading aloud a dorky poem he had written just for her. Somehow he had rhymed "Kendra" in a line about flowers he was going to "send 'er." It was awful, and she had been mortified. She just didn't know how to turn him off. Some days she just felt like killing him. He was such a pest.

The girls ducked their heads and sneaked to a table in the front. The waiter came over with his order pad.

Hallie said, "I'll have a cheeseburger, French fries, and—a Diet Pepsi."

"One out of three." Kendra laughed, and she ordered the same.

Their food came quickly. And so did Rob Prentis. Kendra might have known she couldn't escape his attention so easily. He sauntered over and straddled an empty chair next to Kendra.

"Yum-yum," he said, looking down at Kendra's lunch, then leered up at her.

"Puh-leeze," Hallie said. "Not while we're eating."

"Rob, would you mind?" Kendra was so tense she felt like exploding, but she tried to be polite, even though she knew it wouldn't help. "We're trying to have a private conversation."

"Yeah? What about?"

Hallie said sweetly, as if she were talking to a child, "A private conversation, as in, none of your business."

"That's cool. Don't mind me."

"We won't."

Rob reached over and snatched a French fry from Kendra's plate. "Excellent! A little light on the salt and it needs some of that gourmet red sauce.

Otherwise, you're a great cook." He grabbed another French fry and stared at Kendra as he chewed. Kendra rolled her eyes at Hallie. But when Rob's hand reached out for the third time, she detonated.

"Here. Take them all." She slid her plate over to him. "I wish you'd choke on them!"

Rob took another bite, then clutched his throat and started gurgling. Kendra stared at him in disgust. He threw himself off his chair and thrashed on the floor. He was making whistling, wheezing noises as his legs jerked. Some of his friends came over to laugh at his latest exhibition.

"Gross," Hallie said.

"Cut it out, you kids!" the waiter called. "You want to fool around, take it outside." He walked up to the group watching Rob on the floor.

"Hey! He's turning blue!" one of his friends shouted.

Kendra gasped. Rob's eyes were open wide with panic, and his skin was a bluish tint.

"Get out of my way!" the waiter said. He yanked Rob up from the floor and grabbed him from behind. Pushing hard on Rob's abdomen, he performed the Heimlich maneuver. Each squeeze lifted the boy's feet off the ground. It was hideously grotesque because the two looked as if they were dancing—except that Rob hung limply every time he was lifted. Around them, watching the waiter's every move, his friends were stunned into silence.

It seemed to take forever. But, finally, Rob spit out the French fry that had been caught in his throat. He shuddered and gasped and started breathing again. The waiter helped hold him upright in a chair. Someone phoned for an ambulance. In minutes, the paramedics arrived and took Rob to the hospital for a thorough check, first reassuring everyone that he'd be all right.

Kendra listened to the siren's wail as the ambulance drove away. She was so shocked that her whole body trembled.

She couldn't forget the horrible scene she'd just witnessed. Rob and the waiter had looked as if they were dancing. "Someone who cares about you . . . " A dance with death! The golden stranger's words rang in her ears.

✦ ✦ ✦

Kendra felt weak as she and Hallie walked back to school. She couldn't speak. She couldn't even listen. She hardly heard Hallie rattling on about Rob and his piggishness and how ghastly he looked and how lucky it was that the waiter knew the Heimlich maneuver.

How did it happen? Kendra was in agony—and terribly confused. The stranger's warning was making her sick. I didn't do that, she protested silently. I'd never do anything so awful. No matter how much I couldn't stand Rob, no matter what I said, I'd never hurt anyone. I couldn't! . . . Could I?

Fear almost turned her to ice. Fear—and guilt.

She couldn't ignore the words she had snarled at Rob. Finally, when they reached the steps at Wilbraham, she grabbed Hallie's hand and stopped her from going up.

"Listen," she said urgently, "I have to tell you something. I did that. In the coffee shop. It's my fault Rob almost choked to death. Don't ask me how. I don't know. I only know I did it. I almost killed him!"

"Are you losing it?" Hallie stared at her friend.

"No, I'm serious. It was my fault."

"Kendra." Hallie shook her head. "How could you blame yourself? Rob was stuffing his face like a maniac. No wonder he choked."

She started to pull Kendra up the steps, but Kendra snatched her hand away.

"I mean it. And I'm scared," Kendra said.

Hallie looked into her friend's eyes, then gave her a quick hug. "Look. I know it was awful. It shook me up, too. But everything's fine now. Rob will be okay. By tomorrow you'll have forgotten all about this." She grinned, trying to cheer Kendra up. "Next, you'll be blaming me. I wasn't very nice to him, either. So what if you said you'd do anything to get rid of him. That doesn't mean murder. Besides, you don't really care about Rob and you know it!" She could see Kendra tense up even more. Usually her teasing could snap her friend out of a mood, so she tried again. "Wait! Don't tell me. You changed your mind about Rob and you're actually falling for him?"

"Forget it," Kendra said.

She sat alone on the steps for a few minutes after Hallie headed off to her afternoon classes. She was stung by Hallie's words. Just because she didn't want to go out with Rob didn't mean that she didn't care about him. She certainly didn't want to see him hurt! Kendra couldn't blame Hallie for not believing that she made Rob choke, but how could her best friend think she was so cold? She was hurt and angry.

The late bell rang. Kendra dragged herself up the steps, still thinking about the episode at lunchtime.

Suddenly, as she was walking into the building, a new fear seized her. There had been two parts to the golden man's prophecy. Someone who cared about her would dance with death—and someone she cared about would be lost.

Lost—or dead?

CHAPTER 10

Hallie was waiting outside for Kendra when classes ended. Kendra had promised to show her around the new house today. But now she wasn't sure she wanted her friend to come over. In fact, for a brief moment, Kendra actually wished Hallie would just get lost. Kendra didn't ordinarily hold grudges, but today she couldn't help it. She was still hurt about the way Hallie had reacted to her earlier in the day. Had Hallie just been trying to cheer her up? Was she only pretending not to care about Rob? Or was she really as cold as she had sounded?

Kendra studied Hallie as Kendra walked out the door to join her. Somehow, she couldn't believe Hallie would ever be so uncaring. What's wrong with me? Kendra wondered. How'd I get so suspicious all of a sudden?

"Look at that," Hallie said, interrupting Kendra's thoughts.

On the street below, Neil was talking to Judy

Matthews. Whatever he was saying, Judy was looking up at him in awe as if he were telling her he had just invented television. Total attention was one of Judy's flirty specialties. Her backpack was on the sidewalk, leaving both hands free to run through her flowing hair or to touch Neil lightly to let him know he had just said something brilliant.

"Are all guys dumb, or are they just suckers for blonde hair, big eyes, and a sexy bod?" Hallie asked. "He needs your help, Ken. Better go rescue him before Judy sinks her claws in any deeper."

Kendra appreciated her friend's loyalty. It made her feel much warmer toward Hallie—even if she was still hurt. Together, the girls approached Neil and Judy.

"Where are you two headed?" Neil asked.

"I'm giving Hallie a tour of our new house."

"I hear it's totally cool," Judy said with sincere enthusiasm. "A castle right in the middle of Manhattan! I bet it's haunted. I'm dying to see it!"

"Yeah, when do we all get a royal invitation?" Neil asked.

"How about now?" Kendra asked. "Come on, both of you."

"Kendra!" Hallie said softly, between her teeth, but Kendra shrugged her off. Now or later, it didn't make any difference. Eventually, they'd see the house anyhow. Besides, she wasn't really jealous of Judy. In fact, she actually sort of liked her—she was fun and interesting. She was only annoying whenever there were guys around.

There was much ooh-ing and wow-ing as Kendra led her friends past the construction site on 76th Street and up the front drive. They were as awed as she and Lauren had been when they first saw the house.

She saw Graham out on the grounds talking to Mr. Stavros. They seemed to be walking toward the old shed. For a moment, Kendra was surprised. On one of her earlier explorations of the grounds, she had discovered that the shed was grimy and boarded up. It was obvious that no one had gone inside for ages.

She caught up with the two men and introduced her friends. Graham was charming, as always. He entertained them with a bit of the house's history as they walked. Kendra noticed that Graham occasionally glanced at her wrist. She wasn't wearing the bracelet he had given her that morning— not since she'd seen it in the mysterious photograph on her desk. It was tucked into a drawer, together with the photo, pushed way back. She knew she'd have to say something about it eventually. But not yet. Not until she felt more sure of herself with Graham.

Graham and Mr. Stavros continued walking to the shed. Kendra took her friends across the lawn, up the front steps, and into the house. As she expected, everything fascinated them. She showed them around for a while. Then she left Neil to study Graham's gun collection while she led the girls upstairs to show them her room.

When they came downstairs, Kendra left Hallie and Judy in the hallway where they had stopped to admire a painting of a beautiful woman, an ancestor of Graham's. She went to round up Neil. He was leaning over one of the cases of ancient pistols in Graham's private study. He straightened up when he saw Kendra.

"This is something!" he said. Then he saw the distant look on her face. "Am I imagining it, or are you a little frosty today?" He stepped closer and bent to kiss her.

She didn't stop him. In fact, she didn't even notice that he was kissing her. She was only aware of the sudden faint tinkling of crystal chimes, the unexpected image in her mind of a golden-haired man, and the heavenly feeling of strong arms holding her.

But that had been a dream!

She looked up at Neil in surprise. Why didn't she feel anything? Where was that warm tingle she was used to when Neil held her in his arms? His kisses were usually so warm and exciting, but now she couldn't respond. Why did she feel so distant? Why was she longing for other arms? Other lips?

Neil sensed how withdrawn she had become. He caught her look of surprise, as if she hardly recognized him. "Yeah, it's me," he said, sounding hurt. "Remember? I'm the guy you like to kiss."

"I thought you liked privacy. Do you want the whole world to come in and catch us?" Kendra laughed to cover her embarrassment and confusion. "Let's get a snack," she said.

They headed for the kitchen. Kendra began to open cupboards and check the refrigerator for some goodies. While she was looking, Mrs. Stavros came into the kitchen.

"I was just getting us something to eat," Kendra said.

"You don't have to bother," the housekeeper said coldly. "I'll make you some sandwiches, if you like, and coffee or cold drinks, if you prefer."

"It's no bother," Kendra said. "I can manage myself."

Mrs. Stavros glared at Kendra. "I'm sure you'd rather keep your friends company. Why don't you go into the living room and I'll bring you a little tray?" Her unspoken message was clear: Leave my kitchen alone before you make a mess.

Kendra sighed. It wasn't worth making a big deal about the housekeeper's fussiness. She led Neil into the living room. They flopped down on one of the huge sofas there, in front of an equally huge coffee table.

Judy joined them and started chattering about how awesome everything was. The rooms and the paintings and the gardens and the views . . . everything was just too cool! There was a clattering noise coming from the kitchen, growing louder.

Mrs. Stavros wheeled in a rolling cart. It was attractively laid out with platters of food: thin ham sandwiches, home-baked French bread with jam and butter, plates of fruit and cheese, small iced cakes, and pitchers of orange juice and iced tea. This was her idea of a little tray.

"Awesome," Judy said after the housekeeper left.

Neil cheered up after he took a bite out of one of the delicious sandwiches and ate a handful of grapes. "Beats potato chips," he said. Somehow, he managed to chew, smile, and slice himself a thick piece of cheese at the same time.

"Where's Hallie?" Kendra asked suddenly. She had just realized that there were only the three of them in the living room.

"She went to look for a bathroom," Judy said.

"How long ago was that?" Kendra was flooded with a sense of foreboding. The mark on her hand tingled. Something's wrong. She jumped up from the sofa. "I'll go find her. You two help yourselves," she said, pointing to the food on the cart—as if Neil and Judy weren't already doing their best to empty the plates.

She searched the bathrooms downstairs, but Hallie wasn't in any of them. She ran upstairs. "Hallie?" she croaked. Fear had caused a big lump to form in her throat. There was no answer. She knocked on the bathroom doors on the other floors, calling Hallie's name. When she got no answer, she opened the doors and found the bathrooms empty. She hurried downstairs again. With every second that passed, her feeling of dread grew.

I mustn't panic, she told herself.

"Hallie?" she called from the front hall. Then louder.

Neil and Judy joined her. They had heard the anxiety in her voice.

"I can't find her," Kendra said desperately.

"What's going on?" Anthony asked. He was just coming in the front door when he saw the worried group in the hall.

Kendra made hasty introductions, then explained. Anthony offered to help in the search. "She couldn't have disappeared," he said. "I'll try Graham's study, and you check the kitchen and the back pantry. Your friend may have gone outside and come back in through the kitchen door. Kendra, you better see if she's gotten herself locked into one of the closets. It wouldn't be the first time that happened." He was full of purpose and confidence as he sent them off to various parts of the house.

"Hallie! Hallie!" Their calls echoed in the marble-floored halls and from the back rooms. But there was no sign of Hallie.

When they regrouped, Anthony sent them off again, like military troops, to search the upper floors.

Coming down the stairs again, Kendra was almost choking with fear. Then she had a sudden blazing thought: the underground tunnels. Why didn't Anthony suggest they check the maze of corridors that opened off the main floor? Was he deliberately steering them away from the door that led to the maze? I must be imagining things. But the more Anthony directed them to other parts of the house, the surer she was that he was preventing them from checking behind that door. Why?

The group gathered again in the front hall, without Hallie. Kendra was trying to control her growing frenzy.

"Anthony, what about the underground passageway?" she asked him. "Maybe that's where she went."

"Impossible," he said. "There's only one light, and the switch is on the wall, deep inside. You can't see a thing until you get halfway down the first passageway and reach the switch. No one goes in there without a guide and a flashlight. Would you?" he challenged her.

"N-no," she answered, fearfully recalling that first day when he showed them through the dark, horrible tunnels.

"I'm sure your friend isn't that dumb, either," he said. Clearly he didn't want Kendra looking through the hidden corridors of the maze. Kendra was sure of it now. She had to think of a way to get away from Anthony and continue searching for Hallie.

"Well, maybe she's outside," Kendra suggested. "Let's check. You two come, too." Neil and Judy followed Anthony to the front door.

As they were leaving the house, Kendra hung back and let them go without her.

Quickly, before anyone could stop her, she retraced her steps and returned to the forbidden door—the door that led into the loathsome maze. She didn't really want to enter. But she had to.

Breathlessly, she pushed the door open—then stopped as the disgusting air wafted out. It smelled of wetness and decay.

I can't! she thought. She was paralyzed with terror. The dark, twisting passages stretched out beyond the door. It was pitch-black inside—too dark to see anything. But she felt the corridors as if they were a living thing, an evil presence.

I'm too scared. What would she find in there? She was too frightened to move.

I must! she told herself. I have to do it, for Hallie's sake.

She was panting as she forced herself to plunge inside and take a few fearful steps.

"Hallie?" she whispered breathlessly.

There was no answer.

Feeling with her hands along the walls, Kendra continued to whisper her friend's name. Slowly, she moved deeper into the tunnel. It was black and oppressive, like a cave. The air grew heavier, the walls felt damp, almost slimy. Maybe she could find the light switch Anthony had mentioned.

"Hallie?" she called, louder now. Her voice shook with fear. The name echoed through the hallway. But still there was no answer.

The further she went, the colder it became. Kendra was shivering now—but not just from the cold. Terror was closing in around her. The mark on her hand was throbbing. She wanted to go back. She had to get out of there!

Just as she was about to turn back, her foot slid forward and touched something soft. She stopped, petrified. She felt sick. But she had to know. She knelt down.

It was Hallie.

She was lying in a heap on the floor.

She wasn't moving.

Kendra's hand flew over her mouth in horror. She's dead!

✦ ✦ ✦

Kendra's screams reverberated through the tunnel. They echoed off the slick, damp walls. The marble floors of the main hall magnified the sound and carried it out to the grounds around the house. It was only a matter of minutes before the others came running down the passageway, shouting. The panic in their voices matched the horror in Kendra's. They gathered around her as she knelt next to the body of their friend.

"What happened?" Anthony asked. He reached up and felt along the wall. He found the switch and turned it on. A dim light shone down on them—on the body lying on the stone floor. Kendra had been standing right under the switch when she found Hallie.

"I d-don't know," Kendra said. The words came out trembling. "An accident. Something awful. It's Hallie. She's—she's . . ." Dead! She couldn't bear to say the word out loud. She stood and backed up against the slimy wall.

Judy leaned against Neil, sobbing quietly.

Anthony crouched down over Hallie. "She looks as if she fainted," he said.

They all stared at him.

"You mean she's not d-dead?" Judy asked, sniffling.

"No, of course not. Look. She's coming out of it." Anthony moved aside slightly so the others could see.

Hallie's arm flopped out to her side, and she groaned softly.

Kendra was so weak with relief that she felt the tears start to flow as Anthony and Neil lifted Hallie and carried her out of the passageway to safety.

✦ ✦ ✦

"I don't know what happened, really," Hallie said feebly. She was stretched out on the big sofa in the living room. Her voice was no louder than a whisper. "I was looking for a bathroom. I opened that door off the main hall. It was so dark inside. I-I don't know why I went in. I couldn't see a thing. The passage kept turning. I must have gotten lost. When I tried to get back, I didn't know which way to go. Oh, it was awful!" she said, shuddering. "I remember feeling as though something, someone, brushed by me. I guess I fell. I must have hit my head on the floor and passed out."

Kendra felt Hallie's head and checked for a bruise or a bump—for blood. Nothing. Hallie was still stunned, but not hurt.

"I feel like such a dweeb," Hallie groaned. "I can't believe I actually got lost in a house! What a jerk!"

Neil and Judy tried to reassure her. Mrs. Stavros had already removed the cart with the food and cold drinks. So Anthony disappeared into the kitchen to bring Hallie something to drink. But Kendra couldn't stop shaking.

She walked to the window away from the others. She was breathing unsteadily. She had forgotten about her suspicion that Anthony had tried to keep them from finding Hallie. All she could think about was the stranger's ominous words: "Someone who cares about you . . . someone you care about . . ."

First Rob, now Hallie!

The golden man had warned her. Who was he? And what did he want from her?

Whom would he harm next?

Then she had another, even more terrible thought.

When I saw Hallie waiting for me, I wished she would get lost! I wished it—just the way I wished Rob would choke!

A cold chill ran down her spine, and her hands turned to ice. She couldn't remember ever being so helpless—and so frightened!

CHAPTER 11

"What a hunk!" Judy whispered to Kendra. She couldn't take her eyes off Anthony. Even after the panic of the last few hours, nothing could dampen Judy's enthusiasm for an attractive guy. Neil had already taken Hallie home. Judy was lingering just to flirt with Anthony.

He's a big boy. He can take care of himself, Kendra thought. Actually, Anthony seemed pleased by the attention.

Lauren walked into the living room, crunching on a stalk of celery.

"Hi, Judy. Hi, Anthony," Lauren said, chewing loudly.

"Hi," Kendra said. "How was school today?"

"Cool! I'm going to try out for a part in the class play next week. Want my autograph now or later?"

"Can I get one now, before you're such a big star you won't even speak to me?" Anthony teased.

Lauren swallowed a mouthful of celery. "I'll always speak to all my wonderful fans. Say, Ken, I heard you make a movie date with Neil for Friday night. What are you going to see?" she asked her sister.

Kendra told her.

"I saw it. So-so. Not worth a second trip," Lauren said.

"Somehow, I can't remember inviting you."

"I haven't seen it yet," Judy said. "How about you, Anthony?" He shook his head. Judy didn't waste a minute. "I heard it was good. So why don't we all go? Okay with you, Anthony?" He nodded his head. "Okay, Ken?" she finally remembered to ask.

"Sure," Kendra agreed. She smiled to herself. Judy was a real master at getting what she wanted. Just like Dinah.

◆ ◆ ◆

On Friday night, the four of them stood in a noisy line outside the theater, waiting to buy tickets. The film was a popular movie about two macho guys out to save the world—but destroying everything in their path on the way. It wouldn't have been Kendra's first choice, but Neil had wanted to see it. And Anthony, too.

Inside, Anthony maneuvered so Kendra was sitting between Neil and himself. Judy was on the aisle, on the other side of Anthony.

The movie started with the deafening explosion of a house. There were bright flames of yellow and red, with flying debris that looked suspiciously like body parts. The audience cheered.

As she watched the film, Kendra had an uncomfortable sensation of warmth. Intense heat was coming from the side where Anthony was sitting. It was unnatural. Then the film's scene shifted. Two cars were racing through the night, down a rain-slicked highway. Kendra felt cold. She shivered and tried to sneak a sideways look at Anthony. But his face was turned slightly away from her, focused on the movie screen.

What is it about him? Kendra wondered. He seemed so natural and friendly. But she couldn't shake the feeling that there was something odd about him. It was impossible to concentrate on the movie. Her thoughts were turning cartwheels inside her head.

Why do I think I shouldn't trust him? Is it because I was so sure that he was trying to steer us away from the hidden tunnels when Hallie was lost? What ever made me think that?

Now, as Kendra sat next to him in the theater, Anthony appeared to be completely engrossed in the movie—and not the least bit aware of her. Still, the weird sensations she felt came from the side next to him. The heat, the cold. Crazy as it seemed, she was certain they came from him. She wished she could see his face. As if the answers would be written there. But he was still turned partly away from her.

Something so odd about him. Odd—or evil? Oh, I hate feeling so suspicious!

She leaned away from Anthony and turned her attention back to the movie. Suddenly, the screen became lighter, almost white. It began to swirl with firefly lights. The delicate tinkling of crystals chimed throughout the theater.

Kendra's golden-haired vision appeared on the screen.

She gasped and gripped the arms of her seat.

The man stared out, eyes flashing, a smile hovering about his lips. He was as handsome and glorious as she remembered. Kendra knew that his intense gaze was fixed directly on her. She was terrified, yet mesmerized, by his beauty. Her hand throbbed.

"Tonight," he said, his voice close in her ear. "Tonight, Kendra, I will make you mine forever."

"No!" she screamed in terror.

She jumped up and climbed over Anthony and Judy.

"Kendra, what's wrong?" Judy asked.

Kendra didn't answer. She ran up the aisle, aware of people staring. She didn't care. She had to get away.

She stood outside the theater, trying to catch her breath.

A second later Judy and Neil burst through the doors. "Kendra, what's going on?" Neil gently laid his arm around her shoulders.

His handsome features were full of worry, and even Judy looked anxious.

Kendra was sorry that she had upset and embarrassed them—and herself, also. "I'm fine," she said, "really." They didn't look too convinced, so she continued. "It was just that I couldn't take the movie, uhh . . ." She thought fast. "All the noise and violence closed in on me. I just had to get out of there. I know it's stupid, but I couldn't help it. I'm okay now."

Kendra saw Anthony saunter out of the theater. He acted as if he hadn't even noticed Kendra's outburst.

You saw how scared I was, she thought. She stared at him with a challenge. Say something.

"Rotten flick, huh?" he said.

✦ ✦ ✦

That night, Kendra was too frightened to go to sleep. She was afraid, but strangely excited, too. She tried to stay awake, but her head drooped on the pillow. When she woke, hours later, she sensed something electrifying in her room. The very air seemed to hum, and little bursts of lightning crackled through the dark.

Laughter rippled across the room, soft and intimate.

He was there in the shadows: her golden visitor sat comfortably at her desk. He was laughing quietly as he studied the photograph he had taken from her drawer. Graham, Helen, and Syrie. Had he known them, too?

Kendra jumped up. She wanted to run to him. She wanted to touch him, to throw herself into his arms. But sudden anger stopped her. Instead she turned on him, demanding, "Who are you? What do you want from me? Tell me your name—now!"

"Hush, Kendra. I'll tell you everything. You must be patient." He shimmered in the dim light.

His seductive voice calmed her. She sat down again on the edge of her bed. She felt almost hypnotized as the golden man rose from his seat at the desk and walked toward her.

"You will know me as Revell," he said, looking down at her.

"Revell." Dreamily, she repeated the name just as he had said it. It sounded like music. "Revell."

He smiled. "I like the sound of my name when you say it."

"Why are you here?" Kendra whispered.

"I'm here because you want me to be here," he said simply.

Kendra knew it was true. "But how . . ."

She faltered into bewildered silence. There were so many things she wanted to ask him, to demand of him. But her nerve failed her, and a strange listlessness stole over her.

"It was meant to be. I've come because I love you, Kendra, more than I've ever loved anyone else. And because you love me, too. You called to me. You summoned me with your longing. I'm here because you want me."

"But what . . . do you want . . . from me?" Kendra stammered.

"Life—eternal life!" His voice rang with passion. "Only you have the power to give it to me. As long as we are together I will survive—and so will you. You are the strongest one, the single most powerful Sensitive. When you came into the world, I felt the promise of a strength more powerful than I have ever known. You are my life, Kendra. I'll never let you go!"

Something in his words, the tone of his voice, alerted her—as if a jagged edge of ugly horror had suddenly slashed through the mists. Kendra struggled to focus her mind, but the picture slid tantalizingly in and out of view. Suddenly her infatuation turned into terrible foreboding.

"No! Don't say that!" she cried fiercely. "I won't be your slave."

"Not a slave! Never! You are too great for that. I'm going to teach you to use your powers. It is the promise I made to you when you were newly born." He took her hand and showed her the mark. "That was the sign I gave you—a promise that I would return one day. And that day is here. Soon you and I will be together forever."

His dazzling blue eyes sparkled with flashes of golden light. Despite her fear, Kendra found herself unable to tear her glance from his.

"I love you, Kendra." He looked down at her tenderly. His hand reached out for hers. "Come to me."

He lifted her to her feet and embraced her. Hungrily, he kissed her.

She couldn't resist. He was even more thrilling than she remembered. She clung to him, dizzy, helpless. She felt as if she were drifting on an endless sea, and time was forgotten.

Suddenly, the mark on Kendra's hand began to tingle. She felt the warning. An appalling terror crept over her.

Danger! Wake up! Your life is in danger!

The warning crashed through her bliss, breaking the trance. It was true—her life was threatened!

Revell was the danger! A greater one than she had ever known. Whatever powers she might have—and she could hardly bring herself to believe that she had any—Revell would swallow up for his own survival. He would take all her strength, then take her life. Panic rose in her chest.

Save yourself!

She summoned all her strength and pushed him away. She stared at him in terror. He wasn't love, he was evil. He had cast a spell on her, and she had to fight him—no matter what. However much she yearned for his touch, Kendra had to resist him. Or he would destroy her!

Revell stepped back. The faint smile on his lips showed that he knew her thoughts. He would wait.

Kendra's head was clearing. She lashed out at Revell in defiant fury. "You made Rob choke the other day, didn't you?" she confronted him. A smile formed on Revell's full lips. "And when Hallie was lost in the passageway, you pushed her and knocked her unconscious. You would have killed them both!" Her voice rose until it seemed to fill the room.

"No, Kendra," Revell said patiently. "You did that. You were angry at both of them. It was your anger that endangered them. I told you, Kendra, you have powers. And you see they are growing stronger. Don't be frightened. You'll learn to control them. I will teach you."

"I don't want those powers. They're dangerous and wrong. And I don't want you!"

Revell shook his head. "It was meant to be. I long for the day when we will be one, Kendra. Forever."

She summoned all her will to answer. "No, Revell! I'll never be yours, I promise you. Get away from me!"

His voice grew harsh. "If you resist, I will destroy everything you care about. Everything you love. Do you understand what I'm saying? Everything—and everyone!"

Lauren! The thought of her sister struck her with the force of a mighty blow.

Before Kendra could speak, the lights glowing around Revell began to crackle. They were disintegrating, fading away. He was growing fainter.

"You can't escape, Kendra. I'll never let you go. I'm part of you now . . . forever. You'll never be free of me."

He was gone now. But his voice lingered in the darkness, whispering,

"Never."

CHAPTER 12

Lauren linked her arm through Kendra's. They had just finished dinner. "Come on, let's go hang out in the garden and talk," she said. "I hardly ever see you alone anymore."

Reluctantly, Kendra allowed herself to be led outside.

It had been several weeks since Kendra had last seen Revell.

At first, she thought he was gone for good. She hoped that, despite all his terrible threats, he had lost interest in her. The mark on her hand had not warned her of any danger.

Still, part of her missed the incredible sensations he awoke in her. When she felt the most painful yearning for him, she fought against it. She would clench her fist and silently order herself: Don't! You must resist or he'll come back, stronger than ever!

Bit by bit, the longing would go away.

But strange things had been happening. Kendra

told herself they were just coincidences. She tried to ignore them. But they were happening too often.

Last week. Yesterday.

Even this morning . . .

Kendra was running down the stairs for breakfast. She was going so fast that the paintings of Graham's ancestors hanging in the stairwell whizzed by like a kaleidoscope. Usually, she liked to linger and admire them. The women were so beautiful in their lovely old-fashioned gowns. The men were so proud and regal. There was one portrait, though, that she hated—a grisly-looking beast of a man with a cruel sneer on his face. This morning as she ran by it, she thought, Ugh! Go away!

To her horror, a spark crackled at a corner of the portrait. A puff of smoke shot out over the stairs. The painting suddenly blistered and curled. It was melting in its frame!

She stopped dead in her tracks.

Don't! she commanded her brain frantically.

The painting restored itself just as suddenly as it had dissolved. But Kendra was shocked. There was no doubt in her mind that she would have destroyed the portrait. Still, she was somewhat encouraged. With a single unspoken word, she had restored it. Now, at least, she was able to control some of her thoughts. The week before, it had been much worse.

She was scratching the itchy patch where her

burned arm was healing when Mrs. Stavros walked by. Before she could stop herself, a flash of anger escaped and flew at the housekeeper.

You hurt me, she silently accused Mrs. Stavros. You saw Syrie's bracelet on my wrist, and you burned my arm.

Mrs. Stavros suddenly cried out in pain and clutched her own arm. Kendra was horrified to see a red mark spreading across the housekeeper's skin. She had wounded her! She hadn't meant to do that!

Kendra felt lost. If Revell were right—if she had the terrible powers he said—she could injure and destroy without meaning to. How would she ever feel comfortable again? Even though she had more control now, there were times when her emotions would escape unchecked and wreak havoc. It might even be damage that she wouldn't be able to reverse, the way she had saved the painting from destruction. She couldn't trust herself.

Kendra had accepted the fact that she was the one who had caused Rob to almost choke to death and Hallie to get lost in the hidden passageways. And what about what happened to Judy the other day?

Judy had been flirting with Neil again. Kendra should have gotten used to it by now. But for one flashing second, it irritated her. Kendra and Neil had just gotten on the Madison Avenue bus when Judy came running up. She started to climb up onto the first step behind Neil. Kendra's anger crackled. Leave him alone! The bus driver closed the door with a snap. Judy was thrown onto the sidewalk. It was horrible. The frightened driver stopped immediately and got out to check on Judy. She wasn't actually hurt—but the fact that Kendra's powers could get so out of control frightened her.

She started to withdraw from friends . . . from situations . . . from people whom she was afraid she might put in jeopardy. From Lauren, especially. And Kendra knew that Lauren was hurt.

"I'm worried about you, Kennie," Lauren said now as they strolled into the garden after dinner. "You're so quiet lately. You used to be fun. Now you're a zombie. I mean, totally out of it. Is it something with Neil? Did you break up again? Come on, what gives?"

Kendra smiled at her sister. She wanted more than anything to confide in Lauren, but how could she tell her anything about Revell and the "accidents" of the past weeks? When she had tried to tell Hallie about her fears the day that Rob choked, Hallie hadn't believed her. Hallie—her best friend. Kendra had to face it. No one would believe her. And even if anyone did, how could Revell be stopped?

Kendra threw her arm around Lauren's shoulder. "Stop worrying," she told the frowning Lauren. "You'll get wrinkles before you're seventeen. My moods have nothing to do with Neil."

"But something is wrong, isn't it?" Lauren pulled away to stare earnestly into Kendra's eyes. "I heard you dropped out of the TV studio workshop and quit your Communications class. You didn't even tell me. I had to hear it from Hallie. I don't get it. You worked so hard for a chance to get on camera." She sat down on one of the stone benches along the garden path and pulled Kendra down next to her.

"So, what's up? You know you can tell me anything." As Lauren pressed her to confide, Kendra only half-listened. Her eyes were fixed on the cemetery at the back of the gardens. Was there a faint stirring among the tombstones? No, everything was calm and still in the balmy evening air.

"You never want to do anything with me anymore," Lauren continued. "Did I do something? You always let me know if you're mad at me. I'm sorry, okay? I don't know why you're so grumpy. Honestly, hanging out with Mrs. Stavros would be more fun."

"Look, Lauren, I'm just tired lately. Please don't bug me."

The leaves of one of the great trees in the cemetery started rustling and shuddering. A large bush below the tree trembled and waved over one of the graves. But there wasn't even a light breeze in the air. And nothing else growing in the cemetery was moving at all. Kendra strained to see if anyone was there.

"I'm trying to help," Lauren said, frustrated. "You're shutting me out. Why? What have I done?" Her voice was shaking. She reached for Kendra's hand.

Kendra jerked her hand away. "If you want to whine at someone, try Dinah, or Graham. Anyone. Just don't push me. Leave me alone, Lauren! Please!" She spoke more sharply than she meant to. She couldn't help herself.

She was instantly sorry, but it was too late.

Lauren jumped up and faced her sister. Angry, hurt tears filled her eyes. "Don't treat me like a pest. You want to be alone? Fine! I don't know what I did to make you hate me, but I hate you, too!" She ran off, sobbing.

Kendra rested her head in her hands. Tears of fear and frustration stung her eyes. She had hardly been paying attention to what Lauren had been saying. Then, all of sudden, she snapped at Lauren. What have I done now? she thought.

No. What has Revell done?

The dry, rustling noise caught her attention again. She looked up. Her gaze turned to the somber grove where Graham's ancestors were buried. She remembered that she had been drawn to the cemetery several weeks ago. But something had stopped her before she got there. What had it been?

Something was moving through the grass around the tombstones. She couldn't see what it was, but she knew that something was hovering around the graves. Something that was silently beckoning to her.

Once again the name leapt into her thoughts: Syrie.

She rose and headed for the cemetery.

✦ ✦ ✦

The evening darkness was closing in. But Kendra quickly found the tombstones that marked the graves of Syrie and her mother, Helen. They were the newest in the cemetery. The light, rose-colored stones were etched with their names and the dates of their births and deaths. In front of each stone, fresh flowers rested in vases.

Syrie and Helen.

A bench of the same rose-colored stone was set in a patch of grass next to the graves. Kendra sat, staring at the tombstones. What a terrible tragedy, she thought. How had Graham and Anthony gotten through it?

In the growing darkness, Kendra leaned down to read the dates on Helen's tombstone. Syrie's mother had been even younger than Dinah when she died.

A flutter of noise sounded nearby. Kendra started. She looked around, straining to hear.

Silence.

She peered again at the graves, reading the dates on Syrie's tombstone.

Syrie was seventeen when she died. The same age as Kendra was now, down to the very month!

Kendra's hands turned to ice. Had Revell chosen Syrie too?

A low moaning rose in the air. It sounded pitiful, like the weeping of someone in terrible grief. Except that it didn't sound human.

The hairs on the back of Kendra's neck bristled. The sound was coming from Syrie's grave!

Kendra leaped to her feet, about to flee toward the house. But something was moving toward her. It was creeping closer. Slowly. She could hear it breathing. She could feel its eyes looking through her.

It was coming from behind Syrie's tombstone, a dark shape, whimpering as it inched closer.

Then a damp body brushed Kendra's leg.

"Oh, Max! You scared me!"

Kendra patted the big black Labrador's head. She sank down on the bench, relieved. Kendra had read that dogs grieved, just as people did. Was Max mourning his dead mistress?

"Let's get out of here," she said to Max. "I've had enough spookiness for one evening."

Max barked as if he agreed.

But as they left the cemetery, Kendra heard another sound behind her. Someone was moaning softly in the shadows.

They both stopped. Max sniffed and whimpered at Kendra's side. He had heard it, too.

"Let's go!" Kendra yelled at Max.

CHAPTER 13

Kendra was scared to death. She didn't slow down until she was halfway across the lawn. She had to stop to catch her breath.

Max trotted at her side as she made her way back to the house. She patted his head a few times. He wagged his tail in response, but without much enthusiasm. Maybe the dog did miss Syrie and knew somehow that she was buried in the cemetery.

Kendra tried to shake off the chill that had settled over her. What had she heard in the cemetery? Could someone really have been moaning? Was Syrie crying out to her?

Is she trying to tell me something?

As Kendra walked, she noticed a light shining in the distance. It came from the other side of the house, on the far side of the grounds.

Max stopped and uttered a low growl. Then he bounded toward the light.

"Max!" Kendra called him, but he kept running. She followed him toward the light.

It was coming from the small shed—the one she was so sure was abandoned. She remembered the day, weeks ago, when she had gone exploring and discovered it.

It had been warm and sunny. But as Kendra approached the building, the temperature seemed to drop suddenly. Something about the shed had caused her to shiver. It was almost as old as the house itself. But it looked as if no one had used it in a very long time. She had tried the door, but it was locked. The windows were covered with grime, so she couldn't see inside. For a moment, she thought she heard soft crying coming from inside. Impossible, she told herself. Still, she had been terribly frightened. Kendra had hurried away from it as quickly as she could. And stayed away ever since.

Now the light in the distance was coming from that same shed. It shone brightly in the dark, bathing the lawn in an eerie golden glow.

Had Graham and Mr. Stavros opened up the old building again?

Kendra felt herself being drawn toward the shed. She moved slowly forward.

By the time she reached the shed, Max had disappeared. Kendra hesitated and felt the same shivery chill she had felt the first time she had come here. She held her breath and listened carefully.

Kendra heard people inside, speaking softly. She

leaned in closer, her heart pounding. The mark on her hand glowed in the light from the windows.

"It has to stop! I will not let this go on! You must stop!"

It was a man's voice, tense and urgent, but too muffled for her to identify the speaker.

"She is my source of power," a different voice said. A much louder voice. "They all were. Surely you realize that."

Kendra gasped.

It was Revell!

She hadn't seen him for weeks. Why had he returned now?

Hearing him speak, the familiar longing swept over Kendra. She hadn't realized how much she had missed him till now. Her thoughts drifted, and she remembered how it felt to be close to him, holding him and kissing him. She took a step forward.

Don't! she ordered herself. He's dangerous. He destroys everything good. She stepped back and shook off the haze in her brain. She thought of her earlier conversation with Lauren. She was not going to let Revell ruin her relationship with her sister. But was it Revell? Or did I do that myself? She hadn't been paying much attention to Lauren lately. She had been too preoccupied. But she was always preoccupied and nervous lately. Because of Revell.

Kendra listened again to the sounds coming from the shed. She wondered who Revell was talking to. Who else could hear him and see him? Cautiously, she crept forward again, up to the door where she could hear better.

The voice was louder now. "You've done enough damage. You must not cause any more pain. I won't let you!"

Kendra gasped. Graham's voice! What was Graham doing with Revell? Did Graham know about Revell's visits to Kendra? Did her kind stepfather have something to do with the horror that Revell had brought to her life?

"I have to know," Kendra whispered. She reached for the doorknob.

"Stop! Don't touch!" a deep voice whispered urgently.

Kendra whirled around, startled. Behind her stood Mr. Stavros, the housekeeper's husband.

He had never spoken to her before. He was grim and quiet as he worked around the house or on the grounds. He would nod in silent greeting whenever they passed, but he never said anything. Graham had once described Mr. Stavros as looking like an ogre, with his bushy mustache and thick black hair. But Kendra had decided he was really very shy. She was surprised that he was speaking to her now, telling her not to try to open the door to the shed.

"Come away, miss. You must please never go in there," Mr. Stavros said.

"Why not?" Kendra asked him.

"The building is old. Very unsafe."

"It looks fine," Kendra insisted.

"No, very unsafe," he repeated solemnly. "We have to seal it, as you see. No one enters."

"But someone's in there now," Kendra argued.

Mr. Stavros looked at her and shook his head. His bushy black mustache shook, too.

Kendra turned back to the shed. It was dark and silent. She hadn't noticed the light go off. Where was Revell? What had happened to Graham? Ignoring Mr. Stavros, she tried the door. It was locked. Had she imagined the light, the voices? No, of course she hadn't. And Max wasn't imagining things either when he ran toward the light of the shed.

"Open the door for me. Please, Mr. Stavros. I know you've got the keys."

"I cannot. You must listen. It is very dangerous. It is not for a young miss to enter there."

Kendra was growing angry and impatient. Again she tried to argue with Mr. Stavros. But he just leaned closer to her and spoke sharply.

"There are things you know nothing about— serious things that can cause great harm. I will not see you hurt." He shook his head again, sadly. "Like poor little Miss Syrie."

Kendra's eyes widened. Syrie? Was the groundskeeper trying to warn her?

"Mr. Stavros, what about Syrie? Did something happen to her in the shed? Tell me, please!"

"Oh, no, miss. A terrible crash of the plane killed Miss Syrie. Such a lovely little one! We cried so much for her, the missus and me."

Kendra couldn't imagine the cold Mrs. Stavros feeling any emotion other than irritation. Still, her husband seemed so sincere. He really wanted to protect Kendra.

Suddenly, his voice grew angry. "Too much sadness here, too much hurting. It must not happen again—to you."

"Why would I get hurt? What's the danger here?"

He shook his head and turned away quickly.

"Mr. Stavros!" she called after him.

He turned back, considering her for a moment. He took a step closer to Kendra and put his finger to his lips.

"Beware Revell," he said in a hoarse whisper. Then he walked away from her, off into the night darkness.

Kendra stared after him, shocked.

What does he know?

✦ ✦ ✦

Kendra tossed restlessly in bed that night. She woke with a start several times, quickly checking around her dark room. She was expecting Revell to show up tonight.

The thought filled her with dread and with longing, a longing she tried to forget. Whatever she did, she had to be careful not to summon him. She couldn't give in to her desires. Once she thought she heard a soft swishing sound in the room. But Revell never appeared.

✦ ✦ ✦

At dawn the household was awakened by a bloodcurdling scream from outside. Feet pounded through the halls downstairs. Doors slammed. Voices rose to join the screaming.

Kendra threw on her robe and rushed down the stairs. Lauren, dazed and sleepy, was close on her heels. Together, they ran out of the house and onto the grounds.

Graham and Anthony were standing on the grass, looking down. Mrs. Stavros was beside them. The girls hurried over to see what they were looking at.

When they reached the group, Kendra looked down and gasped. For a minute, she thought she would throw up.

A body lay sprawled on the grass, face down. A large puddle of dark blood had pooled on the grass under him.

It took a moment, then Kendra recognized the figure. It was Mr. Stavros.

Mrs. Stavros's hand was clasped over her mouth in horror.

Graham looked over at Kendra. "Call 911, quickly," he whispered hoarsely. "Tell them there's been an accident."

Kendra turned to Lauren, noticing for the first

time that her sister looked faint. Her face had drained of all color, and she was staring down at the body, horrified.

"Why don't you go, Lauren," Kendra said, squeezing her arm gently. "Get the police and an ambulance. And get Dinah." She tried to push Lauren toward the house. But her sister was frozen with terror.

"I'll go with her," Anthony said softly. He took Lauren's hand gently and led her toward the house.

Kendra was grateful.

Graham bent down and tried to turn the body over. He was having difficulty moving Mr. Stavros. When he finally got the body on its back, they could see what had caused the puddle of blood in the grass. It was then that Kendra felt the full horror of Mr. Stavros's death. A huge pair of garden shears—giant hedge clippers—was lodged between rocks underneath the body. Its handles were caught in the rocks. Its pointed blades were sticking straight up. From its sharp tip all the way down to the handles, the blades were red. They sparkled wickedly in the early morning light. The shears had pierced Mr. Stavros's neck. "He was murdered," Mrs. Stavros moaned. "My husband was murdered."

They all stared at her, surprised. Why does she think that? Kendra wondered.

"No, no, it was an accident—a freak accident," Graham insisted. "Look at those shears. They're lodged so tightly between the rocks, they didn't come out even when I moved him. Look at the way the blades are pointing up. And how sharp they are. The poor man must have tripped and fallen on them." Graham shook his head. He was in a state of shock.

But, no matter what Graham said, Mrs. Stavros didn't seem convinced by his explanation. The housekeeper shook her head, but didn't say anything further. Kendra wondered what dark knowledge had caused her to assume that her husband had been murdered. She also wondered how her stepfather could be so sure it was an accident. Did he know what really happened?

The next few hours were a blur to Kendra. Dinah and Anthony joined the group surrounding the body. Lauren had remained inside the house. The paramedics in the ambulance arrived first. They were quickly followed by the police. The two officers took one look at the body and immediately called for a crime-scene unit. The doctor in the unit bent over Mr. Stavros for a long time before offering his preliminary opinion: "I think the cause of death was probably a massive coronary infarction—a heart attack. But we'll have to do an autopsy to know for sure. I'd say, from the look of it, he had the heart attack first and then fell on his shears. He was probably already dead when he hit the ground."

Graham nodded.

But even in her dazed state, Kendra didn't believe that Mr. Stavros had died of natural causes. Heart attack or not, his death still seemed horribly violent to her. Had she somehow caused the groundskeeper's death because she'd been angry at him last night? After all, she had injured Mrs. Stavros when she was angry.

I could never have done this, a voice inside her insisted. But, still, she wasn't sure.

The body of Mr. Stavros was wrapped and lifted onto a stretcher. As it was being slid into the back of the ambulance, Kendra heard a chilling, unmistakable sound ringing in her ears
—laughter. Revell's mocking laughter.

Kendra suddenly knew the truth. This is Revell's work. Not yours, the voice in her head assured her. Mr. Stavros tried to protect you. He warned you. And he was killed for his kindness.

✦ ✦ ✦

Graham and Dinah led Mrs. Stavros back to the house.

Only yesterday Kendra had thought that nothing could break the composure of that severe woman. How wrong she'd been. Now Mrs. Stavros was grieving deeply. Her feet moved hesitantly, one step at a time, as if she wanted to turn back and run after the ambulance. Kendra felt the woman's pain in her own heart.

She also felt a fiery rage—at Revell.

He hadn't come to her room last night. Very

well, she would go to him now. She would draw him out of his hiding place. From what he had said to Graham in the shed last night, she thought she knew where that was. Revell was a killer. He lived with death. He surrounded himself with those whose lives had been lost, his victims. She would seek him out among the dead.

Kendra marched with angry purpose toward the cemetery. She would challenge him. She would use whatever she could—threats, promises, the very powers he said she possessed—to make him stop the destruction!

She passed the graves of Syrie and Helen. Her hand lightly brushed Syrie's tombstone. To her surprise, she felt a pulsing warmth. Was she imagining it? She looked around. Soon there would be a new grave and a new tombstone in the cemetery, she thought as she gazed at the other stones. Mr. Stavros would be laid to rest among all the others.

Kendra stopped in the middle of the cemetery under a giant tree. The dark shadow of its leaves blocked out the sunlight.

"Revell! I'm here—waiting," she cried out.

The leaves of the tree rustled and whispered, "Ssshhhh."

"If you want me, come now!" she called.

A faint mocking laughter rose above the sound of the leaves. It was the same grisly laughter she had heard as she watched the body of Mr. Stavros being slid into the ambulance.

Kendra whirled around, looking for Revell. He did not appear. But, suddenly, his chilling voice floated on the air. "Come closer, Kendra."

She started walking without knowing where she was going. She wove through the graves as if she were in a trance.

"Stop!" he ordered her abruptly. Then he broke out into gleeful laughter again.

The sound made her blood run cold. She froze. Her foot had struck a tombstone that was half hidden by thick bushes. She glanced down—and gasped.

She stepped back in horror as she read the name on the stone:

KENDRA VANDERMAN

CHAPTER 14

Kendra fled back to the house. Revell had just shown her her own grave! How could she ever think she'd be a match for Revell? He'd already prepared a place for her in the family plot.

For days, she brooded. She thought about approaching Graham and telling him she'd overheard him and Revell the night Mr. Stavros was killed. But something held her back. She was too frightened. She was terrified that something else—something even more horrible—would happen. Instead, she kept to herself. She moved through her classes like a sleepwalker. She knew she was on automatic pilot and she hoped her teachers wouldn't notice.

At home, nobody paid much attention to her. Graham kept his distance. Anthony, too. Lauren was avoiding her because she was still angry about the way Kendra had snapped at her when they were talking in the garden. And Dinah seldom noticed other people's moods. Kendra was left alone to deal with her own sorrow and terror. She promised herself she'd never go back to the cemetery. She couldn't face the horror of seeing her own tombstone again!

But later that week, the body of Mr. Stavros was returned to the house on 76th Street to be buried. Kendra had to join the others around the new grave for the brief, quiet ceremony. She clenched her fists and would not let herself look around at the other graves. Graham appeared strong and calm as he tried to comfort Mrs. Stavros. But when he turned his head, Kendra could see tears glistening on his cheeks.

As they stood in grim silence around the grave, Kendra thought she heard faint laughter in her ear. Revell was mocking her. She listened and realized that tears had started in her eyes. Was it really laughter she heard? Or was it the wind whistling through the trees in the cemetery? I don't know what's real anymore.

Kendra was relieved when the heavy coffin was lowered into the ground and she could leave.

After the funeral, back at the house, a small suitcase waited on the front terrace. Graham was sending Mrs. Stavros to stay with a cousin in Boston for a few weeks. Kendra was overcome with guilt when she saw the small traveling bag. She was still haunted by the thought that this death was her fault— even though she told herself many times it wasn't.

Kendra lingered on the terrace, waiting for Mrs. Stavros. She had to say something to her before she left. It wasn't long before a taxi drove up and lightly honked its horn. Mrs. Stavros stepped out of the house. Grief was etched on her face.

"I-I'm so sorry, Mrs. Stavros," Kendra said. "I'll never forget your husband. He was very kind to me."

The housekeeper's piercing eyes, now red-rimmed, turned on her. "He was? I didn't know that." She reached for her suitcase.

"Can I help you?" Kendra asked, trying to take the suitcase from Mrs. Stavros and carry it to the taxi.

"Thank you, no. I can manage."

Kendra followed Mrs. Stavros down the steps. The driver took the suitcase to the trunk of the car while Kendra held the door open for Mrs. Stavros. When the housekeeper was settled inside, Kendra closed the door. "Goodbye," she said softly, then turned back to the house.

"Kendra!"

She looked back at the taxi. Mrs. Stavros was leaning out the window.

"Be careful," she said in a hushed tone.

Her ominous warning hung in the air as the taxi drove away.

✦ ✦ ✦

That week, many of the kids at school came up to Kendra, saying they were sorry to hear about the terrible accident at her house. Kendra realized it was mostly sick curiosity that motivated them. The story about how Mr. Stavros had looked when he was found quickly circulated through the halls. But the details had gotten so muddled that everyone had a different version.

"How awful! They said his head was cut off by a shovel!"

"Was he really shot?"

"Do they know who pushed him off the roof?"

Before long, Kendra got fed up with their morbid interest. She was tired of telling them that Mr. Stavros had died of a heart attack, just as the coroner's report had stated. She hated explaining—especially since she herself didn't believe that was the true cause of his death. When Addie Lovell, a particularly irritating girl in her gym class, followed Kendra into the girls' locker room and badgered her for gory details, Kendra lost her temper.

"Leave me alone!" she snapped. "I said I didn't want to talk about it!"

At that moment, a locker door flew open and caught Addie on the forehead.

"Ow!" the girl cried and rushed to look in the mirror. There was no blood, but Kendra could already see the red mark swelling into an ugly bump. She glanced around. No one else was in the locker room. No one else could have flung that door open.

With sad regret, Kendra realized that, once again, she had lost control of her powers. Her anger had caused the attack. As she ran to get Addie an ice pack, she wondered desperately if her life would ever be the same again.

At home that night, Dinah was having fits. Her big party was only two weeks away, and she was frantically searching for a caterer. Why had Graham insisted Mrs. Stavros go away now?

As the days passed, Kendra found herself turning more and more frequently to Anthony for company. He seemed to need her, too. He came to pick her up several times after school and took her to a coffee bar downtown. They talked for hours over cups of steamy cappuccino. Anthony was a good listener. He wanted to hear all about Kendra's friends, her classes, and her ambitions. Kendra wanted to know how he liked being away at college, and how different it was from high school. They took long walks through Central Park and told each other about their past and present girlfriends (Anthony's) and boyfriends (Kendra's). Together they browsed through The Record Hunter and discovered that they liked the same music. Kendra had forgotten the anger and suspicion she felt the night she was at the movies with Anthony.

One Saturday night, Anthony took her to Big Camille's, a new hip-hop club in So-Ho.

"You're a great dancer," Kendra told him as she joined him on the packed dance floor. He was totally wild and full of fun. "Do you go out to clubs a lot?" she asked.

"All the time," Anthony replied. "I love to dance."

As they moved together on the dance floor, Kendra couldn't help noticing how many other girls were shooting her envious looks. She didn't blame them. Anthony was gorgeous and lots of fun to be with. When Graham and Dinah had announced their marriage, Kendra wasn't exactly thrilled about having a stepbrother. But now she found herself feeling very lucky. As the strain between her and Lauren lingered, she was often lonely. So she was especially grateful to have Anthony around.

Still, for all the time they now spent together, Kendra couldn't shake the feeling that Anthony was keeping certain parts of himself from her. Once, when she asked him if he had ever been inside the old shed, he brushed her off, saying that it had been locked for as long as he remembered. And whenever she asked him when he was going back to college, his answers were always vague. He seemed to be holding something back. What was he hiding?

She wished he would open up. He was her only link to the past. She wanted him to tell her what had happened at the house on 76th Street before she and Lauren and Dinah had arrived. But even if he did keep certain things from her, Kendra felt very close to him. She thought she could ask him anything.

One evening before dinner, they were strolling along the high path overlooking the river. "Tell me about Syrie," Kendra said gently. "It must have been so terrible, losing your sister and your mother that way. I saw a photo of them. They were both so beautiful."

Anthony nodded. "Oh, yeah. I put that picture in your room. You know, I can't remember why I did that. I guess I thought you'd like to see them."

He bent and picked up a small stone from the path. With a powerful swing, he flung it out into the river, following its flight with his eyes.

Anthony put the photo in my room? Why didn't he tell me before?

Before Kendra could say anything, he continued. "Actually, they weren't really my sister and mother," he said casually. "My own mother died right after I was born. I don't remember her. She was very young, Graham told me. Just a teenager when they married, and she died less than a year later. Graham didn't have any pictures of her."

Graham had been married before he met Helen? "B-but I thought Helen was his first wife." Kendra was so astonished she couldn't help stuttering.

"No, my mother was his first wife," Anthony explained. "She's buried out in the cemetery with all the rest of the family. Quite a bunch, aren't they? I sometimes go there to see her grave, but not as much as I did when I was little."

"What was her name, your mother?" Kendra asked.

"Kendra—like yours," Anthony answered, turning to her. "Strange, isn't it? Such an unusual name." He turned away and pitched another stone into the river below.

A rush of heat rose through Kendra's whole body. Kendra! She had never met anyone else with the same name. And now another Kendra had come into her life—her new stepbrother's mother. Another Kendra who was dead. She felt as though a part of herself had died as well. She shivered uncontrollably.

Slowly, she began to realize the truth of what had happened in the cemetery. Revell hadn't led Kendra to her own grave. It was the grave of Anthony's mother.

Kendra Vanderman.

Anthony smiled at her. "I'm starving. How about you? Let's go get dinner." He put his arm around her shoulder and nudged her toward the house.

Kendra walked as if she were in a trance. She couldn't believe what she had just learned from Anthony. Worse, she couldn't stop herself from feeling that something ominous was closing in on her. She felt surrounded. It wasn't just the house, or the cemetery, or all the secrets in Graham's life. It was about death. Death seemed to surround this house and the entire Vanderman family, and it was coming closer. Revell was winning.

✦ ✦ ✦

That night, after dinner, Kendra followed her mother into the small room on the main floor that Dinah had turned into her private study. Dinah sat at an antique desk and shuffled through the many lists she had made for her party.

"I can't understand why you don't want to invite your friends to the party. There's so much room here. They wouldn't have to mingle with my and Graham's guests."

"Not this time. The next party, okay?" Kendra said as diplomatically as possible.

"Well, you and all your friends are going to miss out. It's going to be so festive. I've hired a new groundskeeper, together with his wife, to help out. The caterers have their instructions. And Mrs. Stavros will be back soon. Though heaven knows how much good she'll be. Don't hover, dear. Sit down and give me a hand with this list of flower arrangements. I can't decide which—"

"I came to ask you something," Kendra interrupted. "Could you put those lists down for a minute?"

"All right, if it's that important. What's on your mind?" Dinah looked up at her daughter with impatience.

"Did you know that Graham was married before? I mean, before Helen?"

Dinah screwed up her face in concentration. "He might have mentioned it. Yes, I think he did, but he said it was so long ago and it lasted such a short time, not even a year, and she was just a child. Everyone married so young in those days. I'm sure he told me. I must have forgotten."

"Anthony was her son, not Helen's."

"Really? I didn't know that."

"Did Graham tell you her name?" The look on Dinah's face told Kendra that he hadn't. "Her name was Kendra."

Dinah blinked. "Well, isn't that a coincidence! I've never met another Kendra—have you? It's such an uncommon name. It was your father's choice. I think it was the name of a great-aunt he was very fond of. How strange!"

"Don't you think it's even stranger that Graham didn't mention it?"

"Of course not! You know we had such a whirlwind courtship, there was so much else to talk about, such a short time—a simple little thing like a name, why would he even think of it?"

Kendra sighed. "Well, don't you think it's unusual that both of Graham's previous wives died—Helen in an accident, and his first wife I don't know how? Isn't that a little weird?"

"Oh, dear, are you worrying about me?" Dinah laughed. "You mustn't be superstitious. Nothing's going to happen to me. We're all the same family now, and we're going to be together for a long time. I must say I'm glad to see you getting along so well with Anthony. And with Graham, too. He's very fond of you. And of Lauren, of course. But I think you're his favorite. He showed me the lovely bracelet he gave you. Come to think of it, I never see you wearing it. Didn't you like it?"

Kendra stared at her mother. She wanted to say, It was Syrie's bracelet, and Syrie died. Why did Graham give it to me? Instead, she remained silent. For whatever reason, Dinah didn't seem the least bit curious about Graham's past.

"I hope you thanked him properly," Dinah continued, oblivious to Kendra's distress.

Kendra shrugged. "Of course I did. It's just a little fancy to wear to school."

"You must be careful not to hurt Graham's feelings when he's trying so hard to be nice to you, Kendra. I think you should make an effort to please him."

"Don't worry, I will," Kendra said. She sighed as she left Dinah buried in her lists again. Trying to involve her mother in her problems was utterly hopeless. Whatever was going on here, Kendra would have to deal with it alone. There was no one she could turn to for help. Kendra only hoped she'd use her power to protect her mother and Lauren, if and when they needed it.

✦ ✦ ✦

The weather was beautiful the following afternoon—perfect for the softball game in Central Park. It was Wilbraham Academy against P.S. 12, an old rival. The public school had some terrific jocks. But Judy Matthews was a wicked pitcher and Neil Jarmon could whack the ball almost out of the park. They were Wilbraham's stars.

Kendra was on the team, too. She wasn't exactly a star, but she managed second base pretty well. And she wouldn't let her team down by dropping out, no matter how distracted and exhausted she felt. She joined the others, lugging bats and balls out onto the field.

A crowd of kids sat on the grass, watching. Kendra spotted Anthony, Lauren, and Hallie sitting together near Rob Prentis and his friends. As usual, Rob was clowning around, rolling on the grass, but for once Kendra was glad to see him acting up. She still felt guilty and haunted over the choking incident.

Kendra was also glad to see Lauren at the game. Lauren was still very cold to her—the two of them never talked anymore—but at least she had come to cheer for Kendra's team.

The game moved slowly. There were lots of walks and strikeouts. For the first four innings, the score was one-zip, in favor of P.S. 12.

Things picked up by the fifth inning. Wilbraham was up at bat. Kendra had gotten herself to first base, and her teammates got hits that moved her to third. The bases were loaded. The kids rooting from the sidelines were going wild.

As the opposing pitcher stepped up to the mound, Kendra looked to see whether Lauren was watching. She spotted Anthony with Hallie, but she didn't see her sister. Her eyes scanned the sidelines.

A little way off, Lauren was leaning against a tree, talking to a man—a tall, handsome, blond man. It was Revell!

Oh, no! Lauren, get away! Run!

Kendra looked around desperately. She couldn't move.

Run! Lauren, run!

"Run! Kendra, run!" From the field and the sidelines, her teammates were screaming at her. The Wilbraham player at bat had hit a soaring ball to the outfield and was heading for first base. Kendra was rooted at third. The runners piled up behind her, and it was one-two-three outs.

Everyone groaned, but Kendra hardly noticed as she raced off the field.

Lauren stood under the tree, alone now. She watched without expression as Kendra ran up to her.

"Looks like it's back to the minors for you," Lauren said coldly.

"Who were you talking to a minute ago?" Kendra asked, ignoring Lauren's dig.

"Search me. Maybe a scout for the Mets?"

"Cut it out, Lauren. I'm serious. Do you know that man who was standing here with you? What did he want?"

Lauren turned on her angrily. "Look, I'm really honored that you feel like talking to me now. But it's none of your business if I want to have a conversation with someone. How should I know who he was? The guy just came up and asked me the time and made some dumb remark about the game. I suppose you think he was going to offer me a lollipop and kidnap me, right?"

"Oh, Lauren, you could get yourself into so much trouble, don't you realize that? Please, don't be a fool."

"What? For talking to a perfectly pleasant guy? In the middle of a crowd? Give me a little credit, would you? And quit trying to run my life! You're not my mother!"

She looked at Kendra with disgust. Then she turned and walked over to Hallie and Anthony.

An icy shiver raced up Kendra's spine. Her worst fears were being realized. Revell could approach Lauren whenever he wished. And he would pick a moment when Kendra was in the midst of a situation she couldn't get out of—like being on base in the middle of a game. Revell would approach Lauren when he knew Kendra would not be able to help.

A sudden wild thought seized her: was it possible that Revell was no longer interested in her? That he was now going to pursue Lauren? For one crazy moment, Kendra felt the sting of jealousy. Revell! Had she lost him?

She struggled to control the ache in her heart. Slowly her reason returned.

Revell is evil, she reminded herself. Besides, he'd told her that it was she, Kendra, he was determined to possess. He was taunting her now, reminding her of his threat. He had warned her that her family and friends would be in great danger unless she agreed to do what he wanted. He was only using Lauren now to get to her. He was telling her that she must do what he asked—even if she didn't understand it—or he would make her suffer. But how far would he go?

His grim threat rang in her ears: "If you resist, I will destroy everything you care about—everything and everyone!"

CHAPTER 15

The next morning, a hazy mist rose from the sprawling lawn. Kendra walked barefoot through the dew, foggy puffs swirling around her as she went.

All night she had tossed and turned. She couldn't forget the scene in the park the day before. The sight of Revell talking easily with Lauren chilled her. She had vowed not to return to the cemetery. But she had to confront him. On his own turf.

Everything was deadly quiet in the cold, blue morning light as Kendra left the sleeping house behind and walked to the cemetery. She wrapped her long, white robe closer around her. The mist drifted into almost human shapes behind her as she passed through it.

She entered the cemetery and walked over to Syrie's and Helen's tombstones. A faint glow surrounded them. What was causing them to shine? She rested her hand on Syrie's stone. It was warm to her touch. Helen's, too. She shivered, then moved deeper into the cemetery.

Another tombstone caught her eye through the haze. It glowed with the same blush of light. Kendra knew whose it was. She didn't want to look at it, but somehow it beckoned her. She stepped closer; knowing the name she would read on the weathered stone: "Kendra Vanderman."

She felt heat rise from the tombstone. It seemed to be urging her closer, pulling her down. She bent to touch it. Leaning nearer, she read the dates— then cringed, shocked.

Kendra Vanderman had died at age seventeen! She was the same age as Syrie had been when she died—the same age as Kendra was now!

"Are you surprised?"

Kendra whirled at the voice.

Standing beside her in the mist was Revell. The sparkle that usually danced around him was dimmed by the cloudy air. But still he radiated the same golden beauty that made her breathless with desire.

"Don't be afraid," he said. "I told you, you are different. I'll never let you die." As before, he knew her thoughts; he had read her fears. He smiled sweetly and held out his arms. "Come to me, my love" he murmured.

Kendra tried to stop herself, but she was drawn irresistibly forward. Her feet seemed to have a will of their own. She moved close to Revell and nestled into his embrace. She could feel the crush of his strong body through her thin robe. The mist rose around them like a soft blanket as his lips pressed hers. Minutes passed—or was it hours?

Then a low moaning sound broke through to her consciousness. She pulled away from Revell and looked around in confusion. She was like a sleepwalker waking. The moaning came from all around her. The cemetery hummed with the mournful drone. Revell tried to get her attention again. He stroked her hair. He put his finger on her lips and then touched his own. He tried to pull her back toward him.

"Don't!" she commanded, breaking away. She had finally found some inner strength. The moaning stopped abruptly.

"Why are you fighting me?" he asked.

"Stay away from me," Kendra said angrily. "And stay away from Lauren! I saw you with her yesterday, talking in the park. What did she see when she looked at you? Can she see you as you are—as I see you? Or did you put her in a trance so that you looked different? Whatever she saw, don't ever go near her again. I won't let you harm my sister! I'll kill you first! I swear it, Revell."

Revell laughed. "My name is sweet on your lips." He reached for her hand, but she snatched it away.

"You killed Mr. Stavros," she stormed at him. "I know it. I heard you laughing at his funeral. How can you be so cruel? He never harmed you."

"But he would have. He was interfering with my plans."

"Your plans for me? All the poor man did was try to warn me about you. What kind of strength did he have against you?"

"No one interferes with my life." His voice had a harsh edge. "I won't permit it."

"Did you kill Syrie and Helen—and Anthony's mother, too? How many people have you murdered? Am I going to be next?"

"I told you, I'd never let you die. You are the special Sensitive one I've waited for. All these endless years, I've waited just for you, Kendra."

She glared at him. "What do you want from me?"

He sighed. "I'll tell you. I have no choice. You are stronger than the others, and you can understand more."

"I don't understand anything." She shook her head. "Except that you've come to kill."

"No, that's wrong. I come to bring life, eternal life. And love. Kendra, you are the source of my power. I am here to help you grow and develop your gifts. It's your power that feeds me, that keeps me alive. You are the reason I exist."

"That's horrible!" Kendra cried.

"Wait." Revell held up a hand to halt her. "Listen to what I'm saying. As you give me immortal life, I will share it with you. Soon, when you let me love you, we'll be together for all eternity. You will forget about everything here in this simple world of your present life. Nothing will matter but our existence together. You will live with me—forever, in a timeless world where my love surrounds you with glory!"

"That's crazy! I don't want that kind of life. And I don't want you. Do you think I would ever trust you? If I help you survive, what next? Then you'll kill me?"

"No. Not the eternal you."

His voice was suddenly so menacing that Kendra trembled.

"Look. Over there." Revell pointed to the edge of the cemetery.

A ghostly figure hovered over the tombstones that marked the graves of Syrie and Helen. Kendra could barely see it, it was so faint. It was a young girl, shimmering in the soft morning light. Slowly, she raised her transparent phantom arms in a gesture of pleading toward Kendra. Was it Syrie?

Kendra peered through the mist. No! That long blonde hair! That face! It wasn't Syrie. It was Lauren! Lauren as a specter. Lauren dead.

"No! Stop it!"

The ghost vanished into the vapor.

Kendra whirled back to Revell. "You can't touch her. I beg you, Revell. With all my heart, I'm pleading with you. Please don't hurt Lauren. I'll do whatever you want," she said softly, "as long as you leave her alone."

I'll do anything, she vowed silently.

He watched her for a moment, then shook his

head. "You don't have to do anything, Kendra," he whispered. "Just say you'll be mine. Let me live in you."

Kendra closed her eyes and said nothing. She felt him leave.

Then she sank to her knees at the base of Kendra Vanderman's tombstone and wept as the mist closed in around her.

CHAPTER 16

Kendra staggered in from the garden just as
Lauren was opening the front door. Her white robe
was stained with grass and soil, and her face was
stained with tears.

Lauren gasped at her sister's shocking appear-
ance. For a minute, she forgot about being angry.
"Kennie! Are you hurt? What happened to you?"

"Nothing," Kendra answered, forcing a smile.

Lauren was getting ready for her early morning
horseback ride. She was dressed in riding jodh-
purs, and her long blonde hair fell from below her
hard, black hat. "Nothing?" she asked, staring at
Kendra.

"I'm fine—really," Kendra said. "I just went for
a walk outside and tripped. Cut my knee. No big
deal. I'd better go put something on it." She headed for the stairs.

"Oh, sure," Lauren said, calling after Kendra.
"No big deal? You come in looking like one of the
construction steamrollers ran over you, and it's,

like, nothing happened. Excuse me for caring!"
She slammed the front door on her way out.

I've done it again. Kendra sighed. It seemed that things would never be the same again between her and Lauren. But how could she explain to Lauren what had really happened? How could Kendra explain Revell—how he had entered her life, how he'd drawn her to him, how he wanted her to surrender herself to him. And how he now wanted to destroy everyone and everything close to her? What could she possibly say that would make Lauren understand all that had happened?

Rebellion filled her heart. She felt the blood pound in her ears. Angry tears streamed down her face.

I won't let you take Lauren from me. I'll fight you, Revell. Whatever it takes, you won't win!

✦ ✦ ✦

The phone in her room rang as Kendra was dressing for school. She snapped the suede belt closed over her black pants and reached for the receiver.

"I miss going to school with you," Hallie said. "It's no fun walking by myself. I can hardly get myself to my first class anymore."

"Hi, Hallie," Kendra said warmly. She'd only seen Hallie for a minute at the softball game and hadn't spoken to her at school yesterday. "What've you got first period?"

"Another lecture on ecology. You know: the rain forests are drying up, we're running out of rhinos, but the good news is we're up to our ears in alligators."

"I thought you cared about saving the earth." Kendra buttoned her long-sleeved, blue silk blouse with one hand as she talked to her friend.

"I do. It just makes me feel helpless. I mean, what can I do if the rhinos don't want to make out anymore?"

Kendra giggled. "You know as well as I do that they're being killed off for their horns. For souvenirs, for superstitions. It's no joke."

"Yeah, I know, Ken. I didn't mean to sound as if it didn't matter. It's just that every time I hear about people doing that, I start thinking we're fighting a losing battle. Forget what I said. I really do care—a lot. What's your first class today?"

"Latin," Kendra said. She laughed at Hallie's groan. "So what's really up this morning? How come you're calling?"

"I had a cool idea. Why don't you move back here, move in with me? We've got lots of room, and my parents would love it. They think you're a Good Influence—capital *G*, capital *I*—and I think you should get out of that spooky house before someone with long teeth comes to chew on your throat."

"What do you mean?" Kendra stiffened. Did Hallie know something about what had been going on at 76th Street? "Why'd you say that?"

"It's grim, your house. And I'm not just saying that because I got lost in one of its dungeons. It gives me the creeps. Don't you miss your old apartment at all?"

"Sure I do. You wouldn't believe how much. But I don't think Dinah would be too thrilled if I shook her hand and said I was moving back to Fifth Avenue and thanks for the nice visit."

Hallie laughed. "Okay. So how about coming for the weekend then? We could hang out and check out the action downtown."

Tears welled up unexpectedly in Kendra's eyes. It seemed like forever since she'd had fun or done something ordinary like hanging out with Hallie. The truth was, she was dying to go stay with Hallie for a weekend. She missed Hallie and her old apartment terribly.

But what about Lauren? Kendra didn't like the idea of leaving Lauren alone in the house, not even for a short weekend. How could she know what Revell might do? She'd have to put off Hallie for now and think about it some more.

"Thanks, Hallie," Kendra said softly into the receiver. "I'd love to come over, but can I let you know later? After I check with Dinah?"

"Sure," her friend replied. "I'd better hang up now and finish getting dressed or I'll really be late for first period. See you later."

The two girls hung up. Kendra stood there for a moment, her hand still on the receiver. She had wanted to accept Hallie's invitation, but right now all she could think about was making sure Lauren was safe.

Suddenly a horrible fear washed over Kendra. She had a powerful sense that Lauren was in danger.

She thought about her sister, and the fight they had earlier that morning. Her heart tightened at the memory of Lauren's anger. But Kendra hadn't lost her temper.

Then Kendra remembered what had happened next: rage had filled her heart, and she had roared out at Revell. For the first time, she had challenged him, threatened him. What had she done? What kind of danger had she put Lauren in?

She heard a hollow, mocking laughter ringing through her room. Revell would have his revenge on her now—through Lauren!

She grabbed a jacket, then raced out of the house. She hailed the first cab she saw and shouted breathlessly, "Balmoral Stables—hurry!"

✦ ✦ ✦

"Hello, Kendra. We haven't seen you in a long time," Henry, the stablehand, greeted her when she dashed through the door. Kendra had never been as horse-crazy as Lauren, but she used to ride frequently, often with her sister. They were both well known at Balmoral. "You're too late to catch Lauren, honey," Henry said. "She's long gone to the park."

"Are any of the horses already tacked up?"

"Well, there's Angel, but she's a little wild this morning. Besides," Henry said, studying her school clothes, "you can't ride dressed like that."

"I'll have to. Please, Henry! Bring Angel out as fast as you can!"

✦ ✦ ✦

Kendra bolted out of the stable on Angel and urged the horse onto the street. She couldn't push Angel too quickly on the city streets. But once she got to the park, she bent low on the mare's back and tore along the bridle path. Angel sensed her rider's mood and flew down the dirt trail.

Kendra heard the shrieking up ahead even before she saw the people running or gaping from the side of the path. A small crowd was gathering.

As Lauren hung on for dear life, Vinnie, her black Arabian stallion, reared, pawing the air frantically. His eyes rolled wildly, the whites flashing with fear. He dropped back to all fours, shaking his big head in a frenzy.

Then, as Kendra drew closer, Vinnie reared again, throwing Lauren from the saddle onto the bridle path. She landed hard and lay there stunned. The people in the crowd gasped as the beautiful black stallion reared again, this time raising his body over his fallen rider. His hooves flashed dangerously close to her. In the midst of the horrified crowd, Kendra saw the leering face of Revell!

"No-o-o-o!" she howled.

Kendra leaned over Angel's back and dug in her heels. Clumps of earth sprayed out behind the mare's hooves as the pair thundered down the trail.

When they reached the spooked horse, Kendra leaned over and grabbed Vinnie's reins with one hand. She had to get him away from Lauren. Vinnie weighed more than a thousand pounds. His hooves were ringed with metal horseshoes that could slice into flesh as easily as if it were butter. If he landed on Lauren, he could splinter her bones and crush her to death!

"Whoa! No, Vinnie! Down! Whoa!" Kendra concentrated her energy on pushing the horse away. She had to free her sister from danger.

The stallion pawed the air again and whinnied frantically.

"Don't!" Kendra roared at him.

With one final shudder, Vinnie came to rest on all four legs—only inches from Lauren's head! He pawed the dirt, breathing heavily. Sweat coated his sleek body. His head swayed back and forth, but he was settling down.

Like typical New Yorkers, the crowd that had gathered cheered. "Way to go!"

"Man, that girl's something else!" It was as if the terrible spectacle had been staged just for their entertainment. Kendra scanned their faces, searching. But as she suspected, the menacing vision of Revell was gone.

Lauren pulled herself up from the ground. She rubbed her side and took a tentative step. She nodded to herself, satisfied that she wasn't really hurt. She was just too stricken to speak.

Kendra swung down from Angel's back, still holding the reins of both horses. Vinnie whinnied softly and rubbed his velvety muzzle against Lauren's neck. Lauren stroked his body and whispered to him. When he was calm, she turned to Kendra.

"Oh, Kennie!" she cried. Without another word, she flung herself into her sister's arms. She was sobbing uncontrollably. "I-I don't know what h-happened. All of a sudden, Vinnie spooked, and I couldn't control him. If you h-hadn't come along . . ."

"Something on the path must have spooked him." Kendra had a pretty good idea what it was. Not something—but someone.

"But I lost c-control! That's never happened before. And Vinnie—it was as if he wanted to kill me or something!"

Kendra tried to calm her shaken sister as her mind raced feverishly. Relief mixed with desperation. She had saved Lauren this time. But what about the next time? Revell would never give her up. If he did, he would die. The more Kendra struggled to escape him, the more he would harm those she loved.

Oh, Lauren, what do I have to do to protect you?

CHAPTER 17

Kendra and Lauren left their horses at the Balmoral Stables and went back to the house to wash and change.

Kendra had missed Latin and the English Literature class that followed, and Lauren had missed French and Biology. As shaken as the girls were, they both agreed they'd rather go to school than hang around the house.

Dinah came down the stairs as they were leaving.

"Good morning, girls. What a beautiful day, isn't it? I didn't realize I was up so early. I don't usually get to see you off to school." She checked her watch. "Hmmm, it must be fast." She continued on to her study without realizing that her daughters had missed some of their morning classes.

Hallie caught up with Kendra in the hall at lunchtime. "Let's eat anywhere but the Mad Deli, okay?"

"Fine with me. Uh, I asked Lauren to come along. Do you mind?" She was uneasy with Lauren out of her sight.

"Sure," Hallie agreed. "So what about my invitation?" she asked while the two girls waited for Lauren. "Did you think about spending the weekend at my place?"

"No—I mean, yes, I thought about it. I'd love to, believe me. But I just can't."

"Can't what?" Lauren asked, joining them in the hall.

"Your sister is no fun anymore," Hallie complained. "I invited her over for the weekend, and she turned me down."

"Why?" Lauren turned to Kendra. "Getting away from Dinah for a few days sounds cool to me."

"To me, too," Kendra said. "But I've got a paper to write and a ton of studying. Besides, what'll you do if I go?"

"Make a move on Anthony," Lauren said, laughing. "That's what you're afraid of, right?"

"Remember, he's your brother now," Kendra said lightly.

"I didn't notice that stopping you. Besides, he's just a stepbrother. No shared genes. Seriously, Kennie," Lauren went on, "why don't you spend the weekend with Hallie? Maybe it'll be good for you—you've been so uptight lately."

"Listen to your sister, Ken," Hallie said. "So young but so wise. Make her say yes, Lauren."

"I'll help her pack," Lauren assured Hallie.

"It's settled, then? I can count on you this week-end?"

Kendra shrugged. "We-ell, I don't know. . . . No, I really can't."

"So, okay, how about next weekend, instead? You told me you didn't know how you'd stand Dinah's party. Next weekend would be perfect."

Kendra looked at Lauren, considering the situation. She really wanted to go. Should she risk it?

"Kendra," Lauren said in a mock severe voice. "Go!"

"Great!" Hallie said, taking Kendra's silence for a yes. "It's all settled. I'll let my folks know. They'll be at your house, at the party. So it's only fair for you to come to ours."

Kendra nodded, not sure what else to do. Lauren clearly wanted Kendra to go to Hallie's for the weekend. Kendra didn't want to have another argument with her.

"Why are we standing around?" Lauren asked. "Didn't someone say lunch?" Lauren linked her arm through Kendra's, and the three girls left the school together.

While Kendra was worried about next weekend, another part of her was happy. She and Lauren were friends again.

✦ ✦ ✦

Coming home from school that afternoon, Kendra was still thinking about how good it felt that things were back to normal with Lauren again. She couldn't help smiling as she passed the construction site on the street at the edge of the Vanderman grounds. As always, the workmen waved, whistled, and called to her from their scaffolds. Kendra was used to them. Both she and Lauren thought the attention they got from the men was actually funny—even if Dinah huffed and puffed and said the workers were rude and sleazy.

Kendra waved back and kept walking.

She noticed Graham talking to a man wearing a suit, tie, and a hard hat. When her stepfather saw her, he signaled and called out. She couldn't hear what he said, but she saw him coming toward her. She stopped and waited.

"Do you think they'll ever be finished?" he asked her. "The architect was just telling me all his problems. Another minute and he would have had me in tears—or asleep. I'm glad you came along to rescue me. Let's go."

They walked up the front path together.

"Your mother certainly is having fun with all her problems!" Graham seemed amused, although Kendra thought that by now he'd want to leave home. "I'm knee-deep in the lists she keeps making. I can't keep track of her plans anymore. Thank goodness Mrs. Stavros will be back soon. Although I wish she had taken me up on my offer and stayed away longer."

"Dinah does need organizing," Kendra agreed.

Something else was on Graham's mind. Kendra could sense it. At last, he said, "Um, Kendra, Dinah told me something personal—I hope you don't mind my mentioning it. She said that the reason you haven't worn the bracelet I gave you is that you think it's too fancy. I hope you don't think I was trying to buy your affection."

Kendra stopped on the path and stared at him. He looked so sincere. He sounded sincere, too. But she had heard him talking to Revell in the shed. What did Graham know? Why was he pretending that no one was in danger? Or had Revell been hypnotizing him? Maybe Graham wasn't even aware of Revell or of the spell Revell had cast on him.

"Have I said something I shouldn't?" Concern clouded Graham's face.

"I didn't think you were buying me off, Graham. It's just that I saw a picture of Syrie," Kendra began. "She was wearing the same bracelet. It made me feel . . . weird. Was that Syrie's bracelet you gave me?"

"Oh, so that's it." Graham looked relieved. "I should have mentioned it. I'm so sorry, Kendra. I wasn't thinking about anything except how glad I'd be if you were wearing it. Yes, it was Syrie's. She loved it and wore it all the time. It was just sitting in my drawer gathering dust. I thought you might like it. Does it bother you that much?"

"I would have felt better if you had told me. It was a bit of a shock seeing it in the photo."

"What photo?" Graham looked puzzled.

"The one of the three of you—Helen, Syrie, and you—standing in front of the house. Anthony put it in my room. He said he thought I'd want to see it."

"Anthony?" Graham frowned. A worried expression crossed his face. He studied her with a look of concern.

Kendra was puzzled by her stepfather's reaction. What was bothering him? Was it that Kendra had seen the picture? Or that it was Anthony who had given it to her? She didn't understand. Maybe Anthony had been trying to warn her—like Mr. Stavros.

She was suddenly fearful for her stepbrother. But when she looked at Graham again, he seemed fine. It was as if nothing had upset him at all.

He took Kendra's elbow and nudged her up the path again, talking slowly. "I'll leave it up to you. Whenever you're ready—if you're ever ready—it would make me very happy to see you wearing Syrie's bracelet. I would feel that something that was so painful in the past has healed, and life can go forward. But I won't mention it again. And you don't have to, either. Is it a deal?" He smiled down at her, but there was sadness in his eyes.

Kendra returned his smile. She remembered the first time she had met Graham. She thought of how he had charmed her with his formal speech—and that same question. He had lost his daughter and his wife, and he was appealing to Kendra to help him mend the hurt. She was moved by the feelings he had just confided in her. Moved, and sorry, too. *I've hurt him. I never meant to do that.*

"It's a deal," she promised.

He held open the door for her, and they entered the house together.

✦ ✦ ✦

The clattering woke Kendra in the middle of the night. She threw on a robe and crept downstairs in her bare feet.

There was no sound on the floor below hers and Lauren's, where Graham and Dinah had their suite of rooms. The floor below that was occupied by Anthony and the Stavroses—although Mrs. Stavros would be alone now when she returned. It, too, was quiet.

As she continued down to the main floor, she heard the clattering sound again, louder. It was like something made of metal clanking against glass.

Max came up to her when she reached the bottom of the staircase. "Good boy," Kendra whispered. Max seemed glad to see her, but subdued. If an intruder had gotten into the house, Max would have been barking wildly. Instead, he nuzzled her hand, wagged his tail hesitantly, and looked up at her.

"What is it, Max?" Kendra whispered. The noise was coming from further away. She stepped out onto the floor and felt the cold marble under her feet. Nervous as she was, something told her she had to investigate. She was glad to have the big Lab at her side. "Let's go see."

The few dim nightlights on the main floor were enough to see by. Together, Kendra and Max followed the noise deeper into the front rooms. A brighter light guided them in the direction of Graham's study. Slowly, they moved toward it. The door to the study was opened only a crack. The noise was coming from inside.

Max stopped. He whimpered once and quivered at Kendra's side.

Kendra pushed the door open and blinked at the brightness. Then she gasped at the sight that greeted her.

Anthony was standing in front of the cases that held Graham's gun collection. His hair was tousled, his face unshaven, and the robe that covered his pajamas hung loosely, sloppily belted. Near him, the top of the largest case was open. In his hand was one of the rare old duelling pistols that Graham was so proud of. Anthony was partly turned toward the door. Kendra could see that he was studying the pistol with a dreamy look on his face. He hadn't moved when Kendra opened the door.

"Anthony!"

He didn't look up.

She stepped into the room, her mind racing. That gun can't be loaded.

Max inched closer to Anthony, but he, too, was ignored.

"Anthony! What are you doing?"

He swayed in her direction. His eyes never left the pistol in his hand.

He's sleepwalking! He's in a trance and doesn't even know I'm here.

Kendra tried frantically to remember what she knew about sleepwalkers, about the danger of waking them abruptly. She crept toward him. She had to get the gun away from him.

Slowly—as if he were moving in slow motion— Anthony raised the pistol.

A golden light swirled in a corner of the room, and the tinkling of chimes filled the air. Kendra didn't dare take her eyes off Anthony, but she knew he was there. Revell! She heard his taunting voice: "No one interferes with my plans."

Anthony's arm rose higher as he whispered, "I'm coming, Mother." He pointed the gun at his head, and his finger tightened on the trigger.

"Don't!"

Kendra sprang forward and slapped the weapon from Anthony's hand. It clattered to the floor—and went off! It was loaded!

The shot woke everyone.

Max began to bark and wouldn't stop. Kendra kicked the pistol out of Anthony's reach and felt the heat of the metal on her bare foot.

"Graham!" she screamed.

Shouting rose from the upper floors. Graham pounded down the stairs into the study, his bathrobe flying. The revolver from his night table was in his hand. Lauren was only seconds behind him. Dinah reached the bottom of the steps and stood there, calling, "What is it? What happened?"

Only Anthony was quiet, unnaturally calm. He looked around in a daze.

"What's going on?" he mumbled. "How'd I get here?"

Kendra dropped down on the couch, her face in her hands. Her whole body was trembling. If she'd arrived just a moment later . . . .

Dinah ushered Anthony upstairs and settled him in his room. Graham put away the gun and locked the door to his study. Lauren carried up a tray of hot cocoa for herself and Kendra. They sat together on Kendra's bed for a few minutes, both of them shaking as they drank.

Kendra could barely speak. All she could think of was the vacant look on Anthony's face, his arm rising so slowly, and the pistol pointing at his head.

Later, when she was alone again, trying in vain to get back to sleep, Kendra heard Revell's chilling laughter echoing through her room.

"You can't protect everyone," he taunted her.

No one is safe, she moaned into her pillow. And it's all my fault.

CHAPTER 18

Mrs. Stavros returned to the house on 76th Street. She looked more tired and anxious than she had before she left.

Despite Kendra's sympathy, she couldn't help being amused at the way her mother acted toward the housekeeper. Dinah said to Mrs. Stavros, "Now, you must take it easy. Grieving takes time— I certainly know all about it. I suffered terribly after the tragic death of my first husband, so I understand perfectly how you're feeling." Then she promptly swept Mrs. Stavros into the frantic arrangements for her party that Saturday and gave the housekeeper a mile-long list of chores.

Graham took Anthony to the doctor for tests. Nothing wrong showed up on the CAT scan and other X rays. Anthony insisted he had had no intention of firing a gun, then or ever. He didn't know how he had gotten to Graham's study in the first place. He was annoyed that his father seemed so worried.

"What's the big deal?" he argued. "It was an accident. So what if I was sleepwalking? It never happened before. It won't happen again."

Kendra wondered if Anthony was aware of Revell. Did Revell have a hypnotic power over Anthony—the same power she suspected he had over Graham? The more she thought about it, the more terrified she became. What if Revell could control anyone he chose, without their even knowing it!

Kendra didn't want to leave Lauren alone in the house for the weekend. "Make a sleep-over date with one of your friends, or I'll cancel my own plans," Kendra insisted.

"That's cool," Lauren said. "It's a bummer here, anyhow." The incident with Anthony had obviously shaken her more than she'd admit.

Lauren rushed to the phone. Within an hour, she had organized a weekend sleep-over with three friends. "Party, party!" she sang into the phone. She seemed like her chipper self again.

Still, Kendra wasn't satisfied. As the weekend drew nearer, the mark on her hand ached constantly. She had the sick feeling that something terrible was closing in on her again. She tried to concentrate on school vacation. It was only two weeks away. Dinah and Graham planned to take them all skiing in Colorado. It would be a great relief to get away from the house for a while—a long while.

By Thursday, the house was upside down. The delivery people arrived in full force. Caterers, florists, and decorators were all crashing into each other. Mrs. Stavros directed the traffic and tried to keep Dinah out of everyone's way.

"Watch it, honey!" Two workmen were lugging a heavy chest up the stairs—it had to be out of the way for Saturday—as Kendra was coming down. They squeezed her against the wall of the stairwell, right under the portrait she hated. She glared up at it for a second. A tiny puff of smoke curled out from a corner of the painting.

Don't, she commanded.

It worked. The smoke vanished. She was in control. The only things she couldn't seem to control were her confused feelings about Revell.

Part of the time, she was furious at him. How dare he invade her life and take away everything that made her happy! Yet when she didn't see him, she was overcome with longing.

And fear.

What would Revell do next? So far, he had threatened the lives of Rob Prentis, Hallie, Lauren, and Anthony—and killed poor Mr. Stavros.

What good are the powers I'm supposed to have? Kendra thought. She couldn't trust herself to resist Revell when he called to her. And she had to be on guard all the time. How else could she stop him when he was on his terrible path of destruction? What would happen if his own anger grew so great that he turned on her in fury? How could she ever hope to defeat him then?

✦ ✦ ✦

On Thursday evening, Graham suggested that they eat out to avoid the disorder of the house. Kendra hesitated. It would definitely be fun to get out of the house. But she had been waiting for a chance to reach Revell. She had to try to reason with him. There must be some way to stop him before things got any worse. Besides giving herself to him.

Kendra told Graham that she had too much studying to do. She'd just grab something from the fridge and nibble in her room.

"My sister the grind," Lauren said to her, smiling.

Just before leaving, Lauren popped into Kendra's room and casually asked her, "Are you and Hallie going to hit the books this weekend, too? If you are, can I borrow your black sequined mini—you know, with the spaghetti straps and the bead trim?"

"Don't even think about it," Kendra warned her. "I've never even worn that dress."

"Okay, okay. I didn't really expect you to lend it," Lauren said, backing off.

"Have a good time," Kendra called as Lauren went downstairs to join the others.

She waited until they all had left. Then she listened for sounds of Mrs. Stavros moving about.

But the house was silent. The housekeeper must be out visiting friends, Kendra decided. She was alone.

"I'm not afraid," she whispered to her empty room.

She pulled on a sweater and went downstairs. Without thinking of where she was going, she opened the front door and walked out into the fresh evening air.

Her long, gauzy print skirt floated out behind her in the breeze. She bent to untie her black ankle-high boots and left them on the porch. If she didn't know consciously where she was going, her feet did. Squishing the damp grass between her bare toes, she glided across the lawn to the darkening cemetery.

Fresh flowers lay on the graves of Syrie and Helen. Kendra wondered who had put them there. Graham? She sat on one of the stone benches nearby and waited. Excitement and fear welled up inside her. A great sadness filled her heart as she studied the tombstones.

Syrie. Helen.

Both of them should have had long lives. Instead, their lives had been cut short by a violent death, sacrificed for Revell's evil purposes.

Suddenly, the two stones began to glow. Around the graveyard, a dozen tombstones began to give off light. It was as if they were beckoning to her.

She rose and walked slowly among them. Some

of the stones were so weathered she could barely read the inscriptions. She hadn't paid much attention to them before. But now she bent to study each one: Greta van Meer. Merrilee Ambrose. Patience Anne Tudor. Consuela Suarez. Frederika Phillips. Barbara Lee Vanderman. So many! All of them were female. And each one had died at age seventeen.

Kendra didn't know what to think as she slowly circled the stones. What was going on at Graham's house? Why had so many women died so young? And why had Revell singled out the women in Graham's family for his evil deeds?

Suddenly, a night bird screeched in a tree nearby. Kendra shivered as the high branches swayed and rustled. A small creature darted among the graves, making the leaves crackle. Kendra hurried back to the bench and pulled her sweater more tightly around her.

Would Revell ever come? She felt so dazed and sleepy all of a sudden. She stretched out on the bench and closed her eyes. Slowly the eerie night sounds faded, and she drifted off to sleep.

She dreamt of the blackbirds she had heard on the first day she came to the house on 76th Street. In her mind, one of them lifted off a high branch. She saw its long, sharp beak and its outstretched, razor claws. She saw its black wings beating as the bird swooped. She could see the scurrying creature on the ground. She heard its tiny scream and watched its flesh being torn into red bits by the big black bird. She tried to cry out. Don't!

"Wake up, Kendra."

Kendra shuddered, and her eyes flickered open.

"You were dreaming," Revell said.

She jumped up and backed away from him. She glanced out over the cemetery. The lights still glowed above the graves. "Look at your work, Revell. You did that. How many women did you kill? I lost count." In her anger, she had forgotten that she meant to reason with him.

He looked at her sadly. "Don't think of death. Think of eternal life—and my love."

She stared at him. His beauty was breathtaking. But she caught herself in time. "How can you talk about love? You're a monster, a murderer." She pointed to the shining graves. "Tell me about your other victims. Were they all as pretty as Syrie? Tell me about Patience Anne Tudor. How did she die?"

He shook his head.

"Tell me!" she cried.

He paused before answering. "She drowned." He pointed in the direction of the high path overlooking the East River. "She fell into the water. Down there. She couldn't swim."

"You mean, she fell off the path? Into the river? How could she have? It's marked so clearly, with bushes and benches."

"It was an accident. It happened at night, on a very dark night. It was such a long time ago, the grounds looked different then. Don't think about it, Kendra."

"I want to think about it, about all of them! Tell me about Merrilee Ambrose. How did she die?"

Revell sighed. "There used to be a barn on the other side of the house. There's an old shed now where it used to stand. It was used to store grain, hay for the horses. . . ." His voice trailed off.

"What happened?"

"Merrilee was in the barn, up in the loft. She was checking the harnesses and ropes. She tripped and fell through the trapdoor."

"The fall killed her?" Kendra asked.

His voice turned icy. "She was holding a harness and had some ropes around her shoulders, around her neck. One of them caught on a board up in the loft."

Kendra gasped. "She was hanged!"

"An accident."

"No! I don't believe that. I think you killed her—all of them! What happened to Greta van Meer? How did she die? The date on her tombstone goes back to the 1700s. I assume she was the first."

"No, not the first," he said quietly. "Kendra, forget about the others. They don't matter. You do. Come here." He reached for her.

She backed away another step. "Why were you going to make Anthony shoot himself? Because he tried to warn me like Mr. Stavros did? Or were you planning another 'accident'? Did you want him to shoot me?"

"Not you. Not my life source . . ."

"Why? Why Anthony!"

Revell shrugged and shook his head as if he could never make her understand. "You can't fight me. Come, let me hold you. I need to feel your power." He moved closer, holding out his strong, muscled arms to enfold her.

Don't!

Kendra inhaled a deep breath and closed her eyes to his beauty. Her fists clenched as she drew herself taller.

Don't . . . don't . . . don't!

Suddenly, she felt a greater power than she had ever known flood through her body. Sparks flashed from her eyes. Her fiery anger blazed out—at Revell, at the sight of all those glowing tombstones and the two sad graves of Syrie and Helen. . . .

With an ear-splitting screech, the stone bench that she had been lying on wrenched itself loose. It rose with violent speed from its base. Whistling with the force of a hurricane, it hurtled through the air and flew at Revell.

He stepped aside quickly . . . but not fast enough.

The bench crashed with a deafening roar at his side and split in two as it landed. But a jagged corner of it caught his leg.

He didn't cry out in pain. He didn't even seem aware that blood was flowing from his leg. He just looked down in amazement at the shattered stone, then at Kendra.

Kendra, too, was astounded. Had she really done that? How was she able to summon up such incredible strength? She looked at Revell with terror. He would have his revenge now. He would destroy her!

His reaction was totally unexpected.

"So, Kendra, your powers have grown so much you can challenge me!" There was actually a note of pride in his voice. "I knew it! You'll be the greatest Sensitive, the strongest of them all!"

She had expected his anger. She believed he would harm her in an unspeakable manner. Her body had tensed as she waited for him to attack. Instead, he spoke with the kind of joy a teacher would feel when a pupil had mastered a difficult lesson. He was delighted with her!

"I'm not your student," she snapped. "I'm not here to please you. If I ever get strong enough, I'll use every bit of my power to get rid of you—forever. Go away! Leave me alone!"

Revell didn't respond. He didn't even seem to hear her. He was staring down at his leg. He had only just noticed it. Bright red blood was spilling from the deep gash where the bench had slashed his flesh. It seeped into the ground he stood on, staining the leaves.

The tombstones in the cemetery suddenly glowed brighter. The soft moaning of many young female voices rose in the air.

Revell looked up at Kendra. His voice came out in a low growl: "Beware, Kendra. Be very careful. Don't try to escape me. You can't. Don't ever forget—I am your destiny."

CHAPTER 19

Kendra staggered back to the house. She could hardly believe what had just happened. Her momentary power over Revell stunned her. She was sure that, for a fleeting instant, he meant to strike out at her—revenge himself by destroying her! She had seen him regain control. He couldn't kill her yet if he wanted to live. Her thoughts spun frantically: what would he do now to punish her?

She undressed, washed, and slipped into bed, exhausted. She brought one of her school books with her and opened it to the chapter assigned for tomorrow's class. She would study in bed until she was too tired to stay awake any longer. She had closed the door to her bedroom to avoid having to see Lauren. Unless it was something important, the sisters honored the signal of a closed door. Tonight, Kendra was in no shape to face Lauren—or anyone else, for that matter. She just wanted to be alone.

Without thinking, she rubbed the mark on her

hand. It was tingling. Trouble. Danger. She knew it was there. The thick textbook for her Modern Psychology class felt heavy in her lap. Her head fell back on the pillow. She let the book fall and reached out to turn off the night-table lamp. She was asleep in an instant. Asleep and vulnerable.

✦ ✦ ✦

Sometime during the night, Kendra thought she felt a light breeze brush her cheek. She tried to open her eyes but she was exhausted. Kendra felt as if her energy was being drained from her body. She rolled over and sighed heavily, unaware of the sound of tinkling chimes fading away.

✦ ✦ ✦

Friday morning, Kendra and Lauren packed their weekend bags to take to school. Downstairs, the main floor of the house was like a zoo. A very noisy zoo. It was cluttered with things for the party. And people, too. They ran back and forth, shouting orders at each other. Graham was keeping out of the way in his study. Anthony was sulking in his room. Mrs. Stavros's lips were tightly closed. The expression on her face hinted that her patience was being tested too hard.

Kendra and Lauren kissed Dinah goodbye at the front door and fled as if they were escaping from prison.

All day at school, Kendra felt tired. She didn't sleep well, haunted by her meeting with Revell in the cemetery the night before. She had wounded him, slashed his leg. She had made him bleed! What would he do to her now?

"Hello?" Hallie said. "I'm here. Where are you?" She nudged Kendra, who stood deep in thought in front of her locker.

Kendra turned to her friend. "Sorry, Hallie. I didn't get much sleep last night."

Hallie sighed. "Oh, terrific! You're going to be fun company this weekend."

"I'll perk up," Kendra promised.

It was drizzling lightly when they left Wilbraham. They decided to walk.

When she entered her old apartment building with Hallie, Kendra's spirits were immediately lifted. The doorman greeted her warmly. The tenants she ran into in the lobby said how glad they were to see her again. She felt warm and welcome—and safe. This was her real home. She hadn't realized how much she'd missed it until she returned.

"You want the bad news first?" Hallie asked as they rode up in the elevator to her apartment.

"How bad?"

"The worst."

Kendra smiled. She knew what that meant. Hallie never missed a chance to complain about her younger brother. Kendra guessed that he'd be around over the weekend, contrary to what Hallie had expected. "Are you still fighting with Jordan?" Kendra asked, laughing. "One of you ought to grow up."

"He promised he'd have a sleep-over this weekend," Hallie griped. "Instead, the brat's going to be hanging around our necks the whole time. We're stuck with him—including tomorrow night when my parents go over to Graham and Dinah's for the party."

"Come on, he's not as bad as all that," Kendra told her. "He's awfully smart and cute, even if he is a little nerdy. I like him."

"He's yours! One week, and you'd be cured. I just don't want him bugging us."

"He doesn't bug me."

"You only like him because he worships you."

"Exactly." Kendra grinned.

Hallie grumbled in reply as she unlocked her front door. The two girls walked inside and dumped their school books and Kendra's weekend bag on the floor.

A small, freckled, redheaded boy came out of the kitchen. His face was half-hidden behind a giant slice of pizza.

"Hi, Jordan," Kendra greeted him.

"Mmmmrrff," he said, swallowing quickly.

"Is it possible, Jordan, that you're actually shorter than you were when I saw you this morning?" Hallie teased him.

"At my age, that would be a biological impossibility," Jordan said calmly.

"Time out, you two!" Kendra called. "Knock it off, or I'm out of here!"

"Ask him about his cat," Hallie said.

"You've got a new pet?" Kendra looked around.

As if on cue, a furry orange kitten scampered out of the kitchen and skidded to a stop at Jordan's feet. "His name's Roger," Jordan told Kendra. "Just don't open the door to the balcony when he's in here. He likes to run out and claw the plants outside."

"You should take him to obedience school," Hallie said. "You should take yourself there, too."

Jordan scooped up Roger and teasingly offered him a bite of pizza. The kitten sneezed and jumped out of Jordan's arms. Sliding on the slippery wood floor, he dashed out of the room with Jordan following.

"That's a relief!" Hallie said.

"Let's go out on the balcony," Kendra said. "I guess it's okay to open the door now."

She stepped outside to admire a view she used to love from her own apartment one floor higher. Her family's large terrace had faced in several directions. Hallie's balcony only faced Central Park, so she wouldn't be able to see the East River behind them—or the house on 76th Street. She looked down over the balcony's rail. The light drizzle felt cool and refreshing on her face.

Funny, she thought. When she lived one floor up, Kendra never minded how high up she was. But now, being out on Hallie's balcony frightened her. For a second, she thought she could see something hurtling over the railing—a human body, turning over and over in the air . . . growing smaller as it fell . . . down . . . down . . .

She gasped, and the image disappeared.

"Kendra!" A hollow voice sounded in her ear. She was so deep in the horror of her thoughts that she wasn't even sure she had heard it.

She turned. "Did you call me?" she asked Hallie, who had remained inside.

"Nope. But I want you, anyhow. Come on back in. I need your help. I want to show you my new dresses. I can only keep one, and I don't know which to return."

Quickly, Kendra left the balcony. She was careful to close the door tightly behind her as she returned to the apartment living room.

Together, they walked to Hallie's bedroom and began looking over her dresses. And shoes. And new makeup. And magazines . . .

✦ ✦ ✦

That night, Kendra and Hallie sat on twin beds in Hallie's cluttered bedroom, gossiping. Hallie sincerely loved to gossip. And she was very good at it. By the time midnight rolled around, she had gone through stories and rumors about most of their teachers at Wilbraham—and half the girls in their class. She was ready to start in on the boys. One boy in particular.

"What's with you and Neil? Did you break up with him again?"

Kendra hesitated. She couldn't really say what was going on between her and Neil. She barely saw him at school, and he rarely called anymore. He seemed confused by her. It was as if he didn't know or understand her. Kendra couldn't really blame him for feeling that way. Since she'd moved to 76th Street, nothing had been the same. She certainly wasn't the same.

Now Kendra looked at her friend and shrugged. "I guess people just drift apart," she said.

"Oh, please! I've seen you two together. You're crazy about each other."

"Yeah, maybe." Kendra nodded. She was bone tired and didn't feel like being grilled. "It doesn't matter, really."

"Come on, you can tell me. Was it because Judy was putting a move on him—and he liked it? She does that with all the guys. You don't take her seriously, I hope."

"No . . . it's not Judy . . . it's no big deal, really." Kendra's eyes were closing. She slid down under the covers.

"Okay, the real reason, then." Hallie pressed her. "It's Anthony, isn't it? I don't blame you. He's really cute."

"He's my . . . stepbrother, you nut!" Kendra mumbled.

"Well, living in the same house with him must be totally cool. Do you spend a lot of time together? What does he like to do?" Hallie went on.

Kendra smiled sleepily. Her friend had a big crush on Anthony—that was for sure. The last thing she remembered hearing before she drifted off to sleep was a huge sigh from Hallie.

"Do you think he'd ever like me as a girlfriend? Maybe he doesn't like red hair. I could dye it blonde, or . . ."

✦ ✦ ✦

On Saturday morning, bright and early, the two girls hit the stores. Hallie was always glad to have Kendra's advice about clothes. She dragged her friend in and out of every small boutique on Fifth Avenue.

By the time they finished combing Saks Fifth Avenue, a big department store, Hallie already had a huge collection of shopping bags. Kendra knew that half of Hallie's purchases would be returned the following week. Hallie needed hours in front of her mirror at home to make up her mind about everything.

Kendra had also picked up some cool things for herself—a huge black floppy hat and a super-mini ice-blue silk dress with teeny criss-cross straps. It was perfect for wearing out to the clubs.

When they stepped out onto Fifth Avenue, Kendra squinted up at the gray sky. "It's drizzling again. Let's grab a cab home."

"You wimp!" Hallie said. "Come on! Next stop, Bloomingdale's. I need some makeup, and there's a special at the Lancome counter."

Kendra groaned. "I'm beat, and hungry, too. I'll have to eat a lipstick if we don't get some lunch soon."

"I promise, just the makeup counters—no clothes, no shoes, no purses. It'll just take a sec. Be a sport!"

Reluctantly, Kendra allowed Hallie to drag her uptown to the Lexington Avenue entrance to Bloomingdale's. They were damp from the drizzle as they ducked through the revolving doors.

When they stepped off the escalator onto the main floor, Kendra smiled in spite of herself. She loved the sight of the dazzling B'way Floor—the lights, the crowds of beautiful women and gorgeous men, the noise. The cosmetic counters spread out as far as the eye could see. No way this was going to take a "sec."

Hallie led her through the aisles. They had to dodge the salespeople spraying samples of perfume at them or offering them bonus gifts with their purchase and free make-overs. They had once allowed themselves to be "made over." When they caught sight of themselves in a mirror on the way out of the store, they had burst into uncontrollable giggles. They both had orange faces, gigantic pouty lips, and eyelids heavy with several shades of shadow.

"To the showers, quick!" Kendra had screamed. "Before it becomes permanent!"

"Nah, I'm going to leave mine until Halloween," Hallie had replied.

Today, Hallie was true to her word. She didn't dawdle. She made a beeline straight for the Lancome counter. Soon she had an array of colorful eyeshadows and blushes spread out before her.

Kendra watched for a while; then turned to the less crowded counter behind her. She noticed the mark on her hand was tingling.

A large magnifying mirror surrounded by bright light bulbs rested on the counter top. Kendra peered into it to check her hair after the walk in the rain. She caught a fleeting glance of her face—and then the mirror blazed with a sudden, unnatural light. Smoke swirled in its depths, and another image appeared. She saw something whirling in space . . . someone . . . turning over and over . . . falling slowly . . .

"Kendra!"

The voice rang in her ear, severe and jolting. She started to shake. She knew who was doing this. Revell!

Something ghastly was going to happen. Revell was warning her, taunting her. Someone was in horrible danger! Who?

Not Lauren! Please, no!

The voice in her ear began to laugh. The sound was chilling. Kendra was hypnotized by the whirling image in the mirror. She stared at it frantically. It was a person . . . but it wasn't Lauren! Someone else was in danger right now. Revell was poised to attack. But how?

And who?

Suddenly, Kendra knew.

She scooped up her packages and ran across the aisle to Hallie.

"We've got to go!" She was trembling, almost screaming in Hallie's ear.

"What's wrong?" Hallie asked.

"I can't explain now. Trust me, please! Just come with me now. Hurry!"

Startled, Hallie dropped the eyeshadows she had been studying and grabbed her shopping bags. She followed Kendra on a mad dash through the aisles and out to Third Avenue. Taxis waited outside the store. Kendra dived into the first one and gave the driver Hallie's Fifth Avenue address. They took off almost before Hallie had time to close the door behind her.

Please, don't let us be too late! Kendra prayed as they rocketed uptown.

✦ ✦ ✦

Outside the door to Hallie's apartment, Kendra could hardly keep herself from snatching the keys as Hallie fumbled with the locks. Faster! They had both dropped their shopping bags to free their hands. Kendra felt her heart pounding in anxiety. "Hurry!" she begged the confused Hallie.

From inside the apartment, a small piping voice rose through the door: "Hey! No, Roger! Stop!"

"Stop, Jordan!" Kendra screamed.

At that moment, the door opened. Kendra pushed past Hallie and ran to the living room.

While she looked on in frozen horror, Jordan's kitten, Roger, dashed through the open door onto the balcony—with Jordan in lightning-fast pursuit. The tiles outside were wet from the drizzle. The minute Jordan's feet touched them, he lost control. He began to skid. His arms flailed helplessly in the air. He was sliding across the width of the balcony, straight to the railing. At the speed he was going, in another second he'd be hurled over the edge— out into the air twenty-nine floors above the ground!

"Don't!" Kendra roared. She raced toward the balcony and flung out her hand.

Jordan's foot struck a wooden bucket holding a large tree. For a moment, he teetered on the slick balcony. Desperately, his hand groped for the railing in front of him. At last, his hand made contact. His deadly slide stopped. He was saved from hurtling out over the balcony in a fall that would have killed him!

Roger yowled and scooted back inside the apartment. Jordan just stood there, still clutching the railing. His face was as white as a ghost's.

It had all happened so fast that Hallie was just coming through the front door with their packages when Kendra reached the balcony. Hallie hadn't seen her brother sliding toward a gruesome death. She just saw him now, as he grasped the railing and stared up at Kendra with a horrified look on his face.

"What happened?" Hallie shrieked. At the same time, Hallie's mother came running from the bedroom.

"He's not hurt," Kendra said. Her voice was weak, shaking.

"I—I skidded on the floor," Jordan said tremulously. The tears were starting. He looked up at Kendra. "It was—was like someone pushed me!" He burst into loud sobbing.

Hallie and her mother rushed to him. "Don't cry, Jordie," Hallie said calmly. "It's over now."

Mrs. Benedict knelt and gathered Jordan in her arms. She rocked him as she murmured, "It's okay."

Kendra left Hallie and her mother to comfort Jordan and stepped back inside the apartment. Her knees were trembling. She was more horrified than Jordan.

Revell! You monster!

She heard his evil laughter in her head, in the air all around her.

Punish me, if you're angry! Kendra sent her furious thoughts out into the air. Just me! No one else!

The laughter surrounded her, then stopped. Revell's ominous voice whispered close in her ear: "Next time, Kendra, it might not be a brother. Maybe a sister!"

CHAPTER 20

The rest of the weekend was a nightmare for Kendra. Revell's threat rang in her ears every moment.

She had been a little disappointed Friday when Hallie said they'd have to stay home with Jordan on Saturday night. Kendra had expected they'd join some of the other kids and go dancing at Big Camille's. Now neither one of them minded staying home with him. Instead of partying, they tried on their new dresses. They ordered in pizza after Hallie's parents left for Dinah and Graham's party. Then they all curled up to watch some old movies on the VCR.

Once or twice Kendra noticed Hallie looking at her strangely. Hallie certainly hadn't forgotten their mad dash home from Bloomingdale's. She seemed to be trying to figure out how Kendra had known Jordan was in danger. But to Kendra's relief, Hallie didn't say anything. Hallie must have sensed that Kendra didn't want to answer any questions.

On Sunday, Kendra and Hallie went to the Museum of Modern Art, where a new exhibit had just opened. Two really cute French guys followed them for a while. They were obviously more interested in the girls than in the art on the walls. Finally they invited Kendra and Hallie for cappuccino in the cafe on the museum's terrace overlooking the sculpture garden.

Hallie accepted before Kendra could say anything. But later, as they sipped their creamy, hot coffee, Kendra was glad.

Jean-Louis and Michel were lots of fun and really interesting. And Michel, who couldn't take his eyes off Kendra, was one of the best-looking guys she'd ever seen—and that included Anthony. Both Jean-Louis and Michel were so different from most of the American boys she knew. They seemed more grownup, and friendlier in a sweet way. She loved their accents. She even tried a little of her French on them. It was too bad they were flying home to France that evening. They all exchanged addresses and promised to write and meet again in Paris one day.

For a while, Kendra was distracted. But in the back of her mind, Revell was lurking. His horrible warning took her breath away whenever she thought of it.

Early Monday morning, Kendra rushed back to the house on 76th Street. She had planned to go straight to school with Hallie, but she was too nervous about Lauren.

She expected the house to be in a shambles after the party. It wasn't. Everything was back in order, just as it had been before. It was as if there had never been a party with more than two hundred people in the house on Saturday. Obviously, Mrs. Stavros had been working hard.

Kendra started up the stairs, calling, "Lauren!" There was no answer. "Lauren!" The house seemed unexpectedly quiet.

As she passed the second floor, Dinah called out to her in a sleepy voice from her bedroom. Kendra knocked on the door and walked in.

"Why are you making so much noise?" Dinah complained. She was still in bed, almost buried in a sea of white pillows and comforters. She sat up, yawned lazily, and beckoned Kendra to come closer.

"You missed the most exciting event of the season! What a wonderful party! There were even photographers and reporters from the society columns, though I certainly didn't invite them. Everything went off as smooth as silk—thanks to all my planning. That's so important, isn't it? I—"

"Where's Lauren?" Kendra interrupted her mother.

"Aren't you the least bit interested in my great success?" Dinah grumbled.

"Of course I am. But I knew it would be perfect. Your parties always are."

"Well, a little enthusiasm wouldn't hurt. How was your weekend?" Dinah asked.

"Fine. Where's Lauren?"

Dinah glanced at the jeweled clock on her night table. "I imagine she's getting dressed and ready to ski the slopes in Aspen right now."

"What?!"

"Yes, we changed our vacation plans yesterday. Graham said that Lauren called while I was sleeping yesterday. She wasn't having a very good time with her friends and wanted to come home. He suggested that I let her take an extra week off from school, start her vacation a week early. He said he'd take her and Anthony to Colorado, and we could meet them there later. I thought, why not? So they left yesterday."

Oh, no! Lauren with Graham! Is she safe? Or is Graham acting under Revell's influence?

Dinah yawned again and looked at her bedside phone. "Now, what's the time difference in Aspen? I said I'd phone at breakfast."

"It's two hours earlier. They're probably all still sleeping. I can't believe you let Lauren skip school for a whole week!" Kendra said, stunned.

"You and I will meet them next week," Dinah snapped. "Besides, I think I know what's best for my daughter. For both of you."

Kendra stared at her mother, surprised. Dinah almost never snapped at her. Why was she so irritable today? And why had she let Lauren go away and miss so much school? That was unlike her, too.

Kendra's thoughts leaped back to Lauren. She was thousands of miles away, skiing down slopes that could be risky, sometimes deadly dangerous. Another accident! So easy to arrange. Suppose Revell had arranged for her to be taken away—out of Kendra's reach? How powerful was his control over Graham?

I have to see Lauren—now!

Another horrible thought struck her. Was it possible that Revell was now controlling Dinah, too?

"What's the phone number of their hotel?" Kendra asked tensely.

"Not a hotel, darling." Dinah's burst of annoyance at Kendra had vanished as quickly as it had come. She was herself, and pleasant again. "Graham has a house in the mountains there. Such a beautiful chalet! He showed me pictures. It's very high up, very private. You'll love it. Just a minute. I think I have the phone number here." Dinah flipped through the mess of papers in her night-table drawer. "Oh, I must have left it downstairs. Anyhow, you say it's too early to call. I'll get it for you later."

"Just tell me where it is. I'll get it," Kendra said. She felt her fingernails digging into the palms of her clenched hands.

"You'll never find it. Don't worry so much about Lauren. She's a fine skier. And Graham and Anthony will take good care of her, I'm sure."

"I want to go to Colorado today—right now."

"My goodness! A minute ago, you were upset that Lauren was missing a week of school. Now you want to take a week off yourself? I never know what to expect from you!"

"I want to leave right away," Kendra said. She had to clench her teeth to keep from yelling in frustration.

"All right, if you insist. Just as soon as I finish my breakfast, I'll call the school, and then our travel agent, and . . ."

"Now!"

"Honestly, Kendra. I don't know what's gotten into you. I'm in no mood for a tantrum. All right, go ahead and pack if it's so urgent. I'll make the arrangements now. Just don't shout at me."

Kendra was relieved—for a moment. Then she thought, "Why is Dinah being so agreeable all of a sudden?" She didn't notice the faint tinkling of chimes as she closed the door to her mother's room.

✦ ✦ ✦

Kendra was shaking so hard she could barely get her clothes into her suitcase. She felt she had to be prepared for anything, anywhere—on the walking trails, the ski slopes, even in Graham's chalet—wherever Lauren might be lured into danger.

Dinah had booked her on the next flight to Aspen, which didn't leave until evening. Dinah herself refused to be rushed. She said she'd join them in a day or two.

The hours until the flight were a nightmare. Kendra felt that she'd go crazy. She kept calling the number of Graham's chalet, but there was no answer.

"Well, what did you expect?" Dinah said. "They didn't go to Aspen to sit indoors and look out the windows. They must be out skiing. You'll be there soon enough. So just calm down, won't you?"

But that only made Kendra more nervous.

Oh, Lauren, where are you?

Finally, it was time to leave. She removed her Rossignol skis from the storage closet in the hall. She rested them against the bedroom wall next to her suitcase as she looked around. Had she forgotten anything?

Suddenly, the mark on her hand began to tingle.

Dinah called from downstairs. "The car's here, Kendra."

The walls of her room began to vibrate. Kendra was frozen in place.

A plaintive voice rose in her ear, drowning out Dinah's: "Kennie! Help me!"

It was Lauren! Her voice echoed around the room, calling to Kendra with mournful desperation.

Kendra scooped up her things and raced down the stairs. She paused to kiss Dinah goodbye, then flew out the door to the waiting limousine. As she ran, she sent her thoughts out into the chilly air:

Hold on, Lauren. I'm coming!

✦ ✦ ✦

Dusk was closing in as the car neared JFK Airport.

Kendra leaned forward from the back seat and asked the driver the time.

"Don't worry. You've got plenty of time. You'll be early."

Kendra's stomach lurched.

Late, late. I mustn't be late!

The limo swerved around the ramp leading up to the terminal. They were almost there! She felt that she wanted to jump out of the car before it even stopped.

The driver slowed down as he came up to the terminal's entrance. The back seat of the limo suddenly filled with vibrating light. The driver didn't notice. Nor did he seem to hear the voice screaming in Kendra's ear: "Hurry, Kendra! Help me! Please!"

CHAPTER 21

The limo glided to a smooth halt in front of the entrance to the terminal.

Kendra's hand clutched the door handle. Something made her hesitate before opening it.

"Stop! Go back!" Lauren's voice screamed in her ear.

"I can't! I'm coming to help you," Kendra said aloud.

"What did you say, miss?" the driver asked, turning around in the front seat.

Kendra ignored his question. Her thoughts were only of Lauren. What should she do? Lauren had cried out for help. Now she was begging Kendra to turn back. Was Lauren sending Kendra a warning? Would Revell dare to destroy Kendra on the flight? Would he destroy a whole planeload of innocent people? It was unthinkable. But so was everything else that had been happening.

The driver stepped out of the limo to help Kendra with her luggage. He opened the back door for her before going back to the trunk.

Kendra swung her legs out of the car.

"No, Kennie! Stop! You mustn't get on that plane!

Kendra was paralyzed. Wasn't Lauren in Aspen with Graham and Anthony? Where was she, if not there? Kendra sat half in, half out of the limo. The driver hovered over her, confused.

"Can I help you get out, miss?"

She had the sudden sense that Lauren was much closer—not in Aspen, not far away at all.

"Kennie!"

"I'm not going," she told the driver. "Take me back to the house right away!"

She swung her legs back inside the limo and slammed the door. They took off, with the puzzled chauffeur recklessly breaking the speed laws as Kendra pressed him to hurry. Hurry.

✦ ✦ ✦

Breathlessly, she ran up the front steps of the house, leaving her suitcases and skis for the driver to manage.

Dinah was on the sofa in the living room, talking to a friend on the phone. She looked up without surprise when Kendra burst in.

"Where is Lauren?"

"I'm on the phone, dear," Dinah responded. She didn't notice the urgency in Kendra's voice.

"Where's Lauren?" Kendra screamed.

Dinah was so startled that she made a quick excuse into the phone and hung up.

"I need to know where Lauren is." Kendra was practically pleading.

"I've never heard you act so rude! I gave your sister permission to go out with her friends tonight. I know it's a school night, but she said it was terribly important. Some big opening of a new club—I have no idea where it is. Neither of you ever tell me what you're up to anymore—and she begged me. . . ."

"She's not in Aspen?" Kendra was flabbergasted.

"Of course not! We're all going next week when vacation starts. I told you that."

"No, you told me that Graham took Lauren and Anthony to Colorado a week early."

Now it was Dinah's turn to be astounded. "I certainly did not! Where did you get such an idea? Graham's in his study right now, and Anthony's upstairs."

Kendra felt dizzy.

She stared at Dinah. Her mother was looking at her with a puzzled expression on her face. How much did Dinah know? What was she aware of? Did she know where Lauren was?

She leaned closer to Dinah. "Didn't you make flight arrangements for me to go to Colorado this evening? And didn't you call a car to take me to the airport and? . . ."

Dinah's face was a blank now. She was shaking her head as Kendra begged her for answers.

"I don't know what's the matter with you,

Kendra. This is the strangest bit of nonsense you've come up with in a long time."

Revell did this! He hypnotized her! She's not aware of anything that happened earlier!

The sound of Revell's laughter suddenly burst all around Kendra, wild and cruel. It grew louder and louder, coming from everywhere, echoing violently off the walls and floors.

Her hands flew to her ears to blot out the horrible sound. It stopped, leaving Kendra quaking with terror.

He's poisoned everyone! I can't even trust my own mother!

And now Lauren was gone. What had he done to her? Where was she?

As if in answer, the plaintive voice cried out: "Kennie! Help me!"

Kendra wheeled around and ran out of the living room, leaving Dinah with a totally baffled look on her face. She almost crashed into the limousine driver bringing in her luggage as she raced down the steps.

She stopped in front of the house and cried out into the night.

"Revell! Where's Lauren?"

A rush of cold air wrapped around her and blew her hair about her face. Laughter sounded close in her ear, low now, and intimate—more terrifying even than the crazy raving she had heard inside the house.

"She's with me, my love," Revell answered. "Come to me, and you will see her. Hurry. We're waiting . . . where Syrie sleeps." Revell's voice trailed off into a whisper.

The knowledge of where they were exploded in her heart. She thought she would burst with the pain. Had Revell carried out his threat? Was Lauren? . . .

She couldn't finish the thought.

She took off at desperate speed, flying across the lawn toward the cemetery. Her boots slowed her down on the grass. She pulled them off as she ran.

No lights showed from the cemetery. The night was as black as midnight. But her thoughts were much more frightening than the dark. Terrified, she entered the grove of tombstones and crept up to the graves of Syrie and Helen.

She looked around frantically. No one was there. The heavy air seemed to press in on her, but nothing stirred. She waited for a sound. None came. Her terror froze her blood. Was there a new grave in the cemetery tonight? A new tombstone with Lauren's name on it?

She moved quickly from stone to stone, searching. Her heart was beating so fast she thought she might choke.

There was no fresh grave, no new stone. Standing in the middle of the cemetery, she saw that nothing had changed since the last time she was there. Nothing, except the splintered bench. It was now whole again.

Her shoulders sagged as she realized she didn't know what to do next. Revell had summoned her. He said Lauren was with him. How could he torment her like this? Where were they?

A faint tinkling sounded in her ear. The crystal chimes sang sweetly, and fireflies of light danced before her.

"My love, how could you think I would be so cruel to you?" He rose from the shimmering glow, smiling. He looked more handsome and perfect than ever.

"Revell! Please! What have you done with Lauren? Tell me, and I'll do whatever you ask. Anything! I don't care—even though I know how heartless you can be!"

"Not to you." He held out his arms. They gleamed as golden as the rest of him. "Come to me."

She bowed her head, but didn't move.

"No! I want to know where Lauren is. You said she was with you. Where?"

"Come to me, and you'll see Lauren." His eyes blazed into hers. "You want my arms around you, don't you? You remember how warm they are, how tender and strong—so strong that you want to feel them holding you again. Yes, that's right, Kendra. Come into my arms. One step, then another . . ."

It was as if she were watching someone else. Some other girl, not Kendra, was moving toward Revell's golden light. Slowly, she slipped into his arms, feeling helpless and breathless at the same time. She felt his body sway, turning lightly from side to side, carrying her with him. He was dancing!

Part of her brain screamed out to her: Your sister is in mortal danger, lost, and you're dancing in a graveyard with this monster! She had a wild impulse to laugh. She was afraid she might become hysterical.

Kendra wanted to break away and run. Away from this place, away from Revell. But his touch was so thrilling. The closeness and warmth of his body made her dizzy. She couldn't stop herself from melting in his embrace.

"Look at me, Kendra. Look into my eyes."

She didn't dare.

"Yes, look."

Reluctantly, she raised her head. He was bent so low over her that she could see the golden flecks shining in his electrifying blue eyes. She could see herself reflected there—the pale heart of her face, her eyes wide with astonishment, her long dark hair.

Suddenly, she saw a different face reflected in his eyes. It was dainty and sweet, framed by long blonde hair that spilled to the shoulders. She saw the body below the face. It was dancing wildly as if it were being jerked by the strings of an insane puppet master.

Lauren!

Kendra saw flashing strobe lights and heard the pounding rhythm of a rap group. She saw a sign in neon and recognized the name.

In an instant, she realized where Lauren was!

She also realized something else. Lauren wasn't dancing.

She was being killed as Kendra watched!

CHAPTER 22

"Lauren!" Kendra screamed.

She wrenched herself from Revell's arms and spun away from him. She was gasping for breath as she ran through the tombstones and out of the dark cemetery. Without looking back, she tore across the grass back to the house. Revell's mocking laughter trailed after her.

Dinah was still in the living room when she burst through the front door.

"Kendra?" she called. "What's going on?"

But Kendra kept going without replying.

Barefoot, she took the stairs two at a time up to her room. She grabbed some money for cab fare and slipped into a pair of sandals. Hurry! she screamed at herself as she ran out of her bedroom.

She was halfway down the stairs from the third floor when Anthony opened the door of his room.

"I heard you crashing around upstairs. Is the house on fire? Where are you rushing to?"

"Lauren's in trouble," Kendra cried. "I have to

go find her. It's an emergency!"

"I'll come with you," he said, closing the door of his room behind him.

Together, they ran down the stairs. At the front door, Anthony called out to Dinah, "We're just going out for a bit." He didn't wait for an answer. They were on the street, hailing a cab, in seconds.

"Where to, pal?" the driver asked.

Anthony looked at Kendra.

"Downtown," she told the driver. "To Prowlers." That was the name she had seen flashing in neon lights behind Lauren—when she saw her sister reflected in Revell's eyes. That's how she was so certain she knew where to find Lauren. "It's a new club, just off Astor Place. I'll direct you when we get near."

Instinctively, Kendra knew the fastest route. She had never been there, but she had recently read a magazine article about it. The club was just opening this week. She would recognize it—inside and out—from the pictures she had seen in the magazine. And from the vision in Revell's eyes. She leaned forward to speak, but the driver cut her off: "Yeah, yeah, I know. I saw you running out into the street. I should hurry, right?"

The taxi's crazy dash to Prowlers left Anthony uptight and white-knuckled. Kendra was also tense in the back seat next to him, but her fear had nothing to do with the driving.

They pulled up outside the club. It was obvious

that Prowlers was going to be the latest rage—for a few months, at least. The entrance was mobbed. Celebrity limousines clogged the street. A giant spotlight mounted on a truck threw its blue-white beam of light into the night sky. Long lines of teenagers waited to get in. They pleaded with the bouncer who guarded the rope at the entrance.

Anthony pulled out a handful of bills and gave the money to the bouncer. Kendra hurried to the door, and they were waved through.

They pushed inside—into a swarm of frenzied, screaming, bobbing, panting, sweating dancers.

It was dark and smoky. Red and blue neon glowed from the walls. Strobe lights flashed from the ceiling, blinding them. Over the noise of the crowd, the music pounded with an intensity that made Kendra's whole body shake.

Ordinarily, Kendra loved clubs like Prowlers. But nothing about her life was ordinary anymore. The music, the lights, and the people only made her dizzy. Frantically, she scanned the room for Lauren.

Anthony had disappeared. He had been separated from her side almost as soon as they pushed their way in. Kendra worked her way around the floor. She had to fend off the guys who grabbed her and tried to pull her on to the dance floor. But she couldn't find Lauren anywhere.

Where are you?

She pushed her way through the mob. Tears of

desperation filled her eyes. She clenched her fists in agony and terror. Her thoughts flew wildly in her brain: Lauren must be here! I saw her! Revell showed me what was going to happen. He sent me here to see for myself how he would use Lauren to punish me!

A second later, a sickening thought struck her: I'm too late! He's already done the worst!

Then Kendra spotted a small door to a back room. She slipped through the door and found the crowd in the back room even thicker. She tried to thread her way to a wall so she could lean against it for a moment. Anthony joined her as she rested and caught her breath. He said something, but she couldn't hear over the noise. Her eyes scanned the packed room.

Then she saw the familiar face: Revell!

He was out on the floor, whirling and leaping with a beautiful young girl wearing thick makeup. His mouth was open in wild laughter. The look on his face was intense and savage.

Revell's partner had long, frizzy blonde hair that whipped about her as she danced. She was wearing a skimpy black mini with sequins that sparkled in the glare of the strobe lights. She threw her head back and laughed with delight as Revell spun her around.

It was Lauren!

Even though Kendra had seen a vision of her sister in Revell's eyes, she hadn't recognized her at first. The way Lauren was dressed and the wild look on her face were so unlike her.

Kendra tugged at Anthony's sleeve and pointed. She plunged into the crowd.

After what seemed like forever, Kendra grabbed her sister's arm and shouted, "Lauren, I'm here!"

Lauren stared at her with glazed eyes. Kendra was shocked at the way her sister's face looked under the harsh makeup. Even worse was the hard look she gave Kendra.

"Come with me, Lauren. We're going home."

Lauren sneered at Kendra and shook herself free. She threw herself back into the dancing mob, back into Revell's arms.

Kendra followed her, pleading in desperation. "Listen to me! You've got to come with me! You're in terrible danger!"

She gripped Lauren's shoulders to make her stop spinning. But Lauren twisted away from her again and reached out for Revell. Kendra realized that he had put Lauren under the same powerful spell that he had used on her—and Dinah and Anthony.

She glared at him with passionate fury. "You can't do this! I won't let you!"

He stopped dancing and smiled wickedly at Kendra. She knew it was a challenge: Stop me, if you can!

Kendra felt both her strength and her rage growing with equal force. She violently seized Lauren's arm and snatched her from Revell's grasp. Lauren struggled as Kendra pushed her through the crowd. Kendra shoved and jostled the other dancers as she and Lauren made their way out of the back room. Kendra pushed Lauren through the front area, then outside into fresh air.

Anthony joined them at the crowded front entrance to Prowlers. "What's going on, Kendra? Why? . . ." His words trailed off as he noticed the horrified look on Kendra's face. He turned around to see what she was looking at behind him. "What is it?"

Kendra eyes were fixed on a spot behind Anthony. Revell stood there, smiling his cruel smile. Anthony didn't see him. No one in the crowd saw him. Only Kendra and Lauren knew he was there. Kendra's arms were around her sister. Lauren wriggled as Kendra held on tightly. She was struggling to go to Revell. The sight caused everyone to stare. But Kendra didn't care.

"Come on!" Kendra screamed at Anthony. "Let's go!"

She kept a tight grip on Lauren's arm and shoulders as she raced down the street. She was heading for Astor Place a few blocks away, to the subway. The subway would be the fastest way out—and she wanted out. She had to get Lauren away from Revell, now!

Anthony ran after them, confused. "What's going on?" he asked again as they pounded down the pavement. But Kendra didn't have the time or the breath to answer.

When they reached the subway entrance, Kendra shouted, "This way—down here!"

They ran down the dirty stairs to the even dirtier subway platform below. Kendra didn't let them stop to catch their breaths until they had run the whole length of the platform to the very end. Quickly, she ducked behind a huge supporting pillar and pulled Lauren after her. She beckoned to Anthony to join them and get out of sight, too.

"Kendra, for heaven's sake, what are you running from?" Anthony yelled, frustrated.

"Ssshhh!" she ordered him. She looked over at Lauren. She could hardly bear the sight. She had never seen her sister's sweet face look so hard—so ugly. It wasn't just the harsh makeup. It was her expression. Obviously, she was still under Revell's hypnotic spell. Lauren leaned back against the pillar. She was humming and swaying to some wild music in her head. She didn't seem to be aware of Kendra and Anthony. She didn't even seem to know where she was. Or care.

Kendra peered out fearfully from behind the pillar.

It was a little past three in the morning. The platform was almost empty. Not many New Yorkers cared to brave the subways at that dark hour. Only a few people were huddled together for company in the middle of the platform. Some were reading newspapers. Some were leaning out over the tracks, looking for a sign of the uptown train deep in the tunnel.

Nervously, Kendra eyed the steps leading to the street. She prayed that he wouldn't suddenly appear. Please! Don't let him stalk us here. We'd be cornered—trapped! She turned to stare into the depths of the tunnel and prayed even harder that a train would arrive soon. Now! Before Revell finds us!

There was no sound from the tunnel. No distant rumble. No train yet. All she heard was the rustling of newspapers and the restless shifting of the passengers waiting in the middle of the platform.

Suddenly, she heard footsteps echoing from the stairwell.

Someone was coming down the stairs from the street. Someone with a heavy tread . . . coming slowly . . . noisily . . . with measured footsteps that sounded full of purpose . . .

Revell stepped out onto the subway platform.

They were trapped!

Kendra gasped and pushed Lauren tightly back against the pillar. She mustn't let her see him!

But there was no escaping Revell. His strong voice boomed out, bouncing off the walls of the subway platform: "Lauren!" he called. "Are you hiding from me?"

"Let me go, Kennie! He's calling me! I have to go to him!" Lauren tried to push Kendra away. She struggled to reach Revell. But Kendra didn't relax her grip.

"Anthony! Help me hold her," Kendra cried. "Lauren's in danger!" As baffled as Anthony was, he heard the urgency in Kendra's voice. He ran to help.

Revell's footsteps echoed hollowly as he walked quickly down the platform toward them.

Suddenly, the sound of a train approaching came from deep in the tunnel. It grew to a loud rumble as the train came closer.

Kendra turned to the sound, still battling Lauren. Faster! Oh, please, faster!

The metal wheels of the train screeched as they turned the last curve of the tracks in the tunnel. The noise became thunderous. The platform shook. The train was almost at the station entrance now.

Revell rushed forward and grabbed Lauren's hand. Kendra pressed herself against Lauren's body to protect her.

Anthony gaped at the scene in front of him. Kendra had no idea what he was actually seeing.

All she knew was that the powerful Revell was pulling Lauren out of her grasp!

"Come with me," Revell said to Lauren. His voice was husky and inviting.

"Yes, yes, I want to dance!" Lauren cried. "With you!"

"You will," he said, smiling at her. He turned to

gloat at Kendra. "I showed you where you could find Lauren. To test you. What will you do about it now?"

Kendra held on to Lauren desperately. "No, Revell! I won't let you take her!"

"No? You think not?" An ugly, wicked look came over his face. He darted closer. Moving quickly, he thrust out his arms and shoved Anthony—hard.

With a frantic cry, Anthony plunged off the platform . . . onto the tracks . . . right in the path of the train as it roared into the station.

The people on the platform began to scream and run toward them.

Anthony!

Kendra stood frozen.

If she released Lauren, Revell would lure her away again—maybe forever. If she didn't let go of her sister, Anthony, her stepbrother, would be crushed to death on the tracks!

CHAPTER 23

Kendra felt herself shaking. A massive burst of energy flooded through her whole body. It was the greatest power she had ever experienced. It flashed from her eyes and shot from her fingers. She blazed with the fire of her fury. Holding Lauren tightly, she turned fiercely to the train.

No! No! Don't! Kendra hurled the full force of her power at the speeding subway train. She commanded it to stop!

Sparks flew off the front of the huge metal monster. Flames shot up from the tracks. The brakes on the wheels seized the rails. The train screeched and wailed and slid to a halt—only inches from Anthony's body!

Kendra looked anxiously down into the tracks. Anthony was lying there, dazed. But she could see he wasn't injured. Several people on the platform gathered around them. They reached down to help Anthony up from the tracks.

Kendra sighed with relief—for a brief second.

Then the mark on her hand pulsed with pain and another sensation struck her with wild force: Revell was turning his mighty anger on her!

Her entire body trembled as Revell leaned closer. She was dazzled by the golden lights that surrounded him.

"Keep your sister," he hissed. "It's you I need—and you I will have!"

Kendra recoiled in horror. Still clinging to Lauren, she leaned back against the pillar in the middle of the platform. Lauren was shaking her head as if she were coming out of a deep sleep.

Revell raised his arms over them. "Come to me now, Kendra—or I will destroy you and everyone you care about. I've waited too long, and my patience is gone. You have no choice, Kendra. Do as I say. Now!"

Kendra felt an unbearable pain seize her whole body. She went limp in the face of Revell's force. Tears of helplessness and regret sprang to her eyes. In another moment, Revell would tear her away . . . far from the people she knew and loved . . . away from the world of the living. He would force her into a dark, mysterious world filled with evil and death. She began to sob in agony.

Suddenly, a mournful, desperate voice whispered in her ear: "No, Kendra. You mustn't let him!"

She knew immediately who it was: Syrie!

"You are stronger than I was, Kendra. Stronger

than all of us. Only you have the power to stop Revell. Destroy him! Only you can do this. Save yourself . . . and you will be saving all our spirits."

I—I can't!

"Yes, yes you can—and you must!" Syrie's urgent voice answered. "Do it now, before it's too late!"

Kendra closed her eyes and felt her pain and weakness drain away. She thought of Syrie's desperate plea. She thought of the great power she had felt only minutes ago. She knew if she didn't kill Revell, she'd lose everything.

A savage roaring filled her ears. It raced through her head like the sound of a violent storm.

"I'm waiting." Revell reached for her.

You monster! Evil of all evils! You will never have me!

"Kendra?" Surprise rose in Revell's voice.

Don't ever touch me again! Not me—not anyone. I won't let you, Revell! I will destroy you! Now, forever!

It was Revell's turn to cringe. A startled look came over his face. He backed away a step—then another. Fear flashed in his eyes.

Kendra felt her anger flare up inside her, stronger even than before. Her powerful rage crashed down on him with massive force. With a triumphant roar, she unleashed her full fury at him.

Die, Revell!

Smoke curled from the sides of Revell's beautiful golden face. It began to blister and melt. He howled in agony, like a wild beast. In a flash, his beauty was gone. His flesh was melting. His face was being hideously deformed. Then the flames burst all around him with a loud explosion. He was engulfed in fire. His body jerked. His blazing arms flapped as he danced to the music of Kendra's fury.

Screaming with pain, he vanished. He was vaporized into thin air. Not even ashes were left. Not even smoke. Slowly, his voice faded after him in a last, strangled gasp.

He was gone—at last! Kendra's hand stopped throbbing.

She had won!

CHAPTER 24

They climbed up the subway steps together.

Anthony's face and clothes were smeared with grime from the subway tracks. He was still trembling, but unhurt.

Lauren was in a daze. Mechanically, she followed Kendra up the steps. She was clutching her sister's hand as she had when she was a little girl.

Slowly, they came up from the underground subway into the clean night air. Kendra inhaled deeply. She looked up toward the sky and twinkling stars. She felt at peace for the first time in a very long while. Her strength had overpowered her deadly enemy. Revell's seductive evil would never rule her life again. He was gone forever.

She had destroyed him!

◆ ◆ ◆

They started to walk uptown. Soon it would be dawn—the start of a fresh day. Even though it was a long walk home, they wanted to feel the air on their faces and stretch their aching bodies. For a long time, they walked together, staying close to each other. They were too exhausted to speak.

When the night sky started to turn from black to shimmering dark blue, they hailed a taxi. It wasn't long before they reached 76th Street. They asked the driver to leave them off at the sidewalk, rather than drive them up to the front door. They didn't want to disturb Dinah or Graham with the sound of a car arriving and doors slamming. Kendra didn't notice the drop of blood that fell from the mark on her hand as she stepped onto the sidewalk. The blood glowed in the eerie morning light.

As the early morning sun rose, they trudged wearily up the path to the house. Kendra looked up at its great, dark mass. She realized that she no longer felt that sense of horror and doom that she had when she first saw the house. For the first time, she believed that it would now be her home. This would be the place where she would always be safe.

Kendra put her arms around Lauren and Anthony and sighed.

They were all safe—Lauren, Anthony, all of them. She had protected them. Revell would never harm them again.

She was free!

EPILOGUE

Kendra fell into bed and slept deeply. There were no nightmares to trouble her rest. She didn't dream at all.

Out in the cemetery, muted lights began to glow over the ancient stones. Syrie's and Helen's tombstones shone brighter than the others. A soft, peace-filled sighing wafted in the air. The sound did not reach Kendra's ears.

She slept on.

She wasn't aware of the fireflies flickering in the corner of her room. She didn't hear the crystals chiming. She didn't see him as he floated to the side of her bed and shed his golden light over her still body. She didn't feel the mark on her hand tingle.

She didn't hear him murmur: "Sleep, my sweet Kendra. Rest. You are strong now, but you will never match my strength. You cannot destroy me. You will always come to me when I call you."

Out in the cemetery, a sad moaning rose slowly over the graves. Kendra slept on. She didn't hear the mournful cry. She didn't hear Revell's last whisper.

"Forget me now, if you must. I will watch over you. One day, I will come for you again. And you will not escape next time."

MIDNIGHT Secrets

The Temptation
0-8167-3542-5 $3.50

The Thrill
0-8167-3543-3 $3.50
Coming in December 1994

The Fury
0-8167-3544-1 $3.50
Coming in January 1995

Available wherever you buy books.

A preview of . . .

Midnight Secrets
Volume II The Thrill

Kendra had always felt protective of her younger sister, especially after their father died nearly nine years ago. There wasn't anything Kendra wouldn't do for Lauren.

Except let her sleep away a gorgeous summer day.

"Tennis?" Kendra said cheerfully. "Swimming? A chance to ride Vinnie in the Kentucky Derby?"

Lauren stirred. Vinnie was her beloved Arabian stallion, and the mere mention of his name was enough to wake her.

"Go away, whoever you are," Lauren groaned and burrowed deeper under the covers.

"If you get up now, I'll let you wear my red beaded mini next time we go to a club. The one with the silver fringe."

Lauren sat up groggily and squinted at Kendra. "You mean it?"

"Nope. I lied. But now that you're up . . ."

"Hey, that was mean," Lauren declared.

"I know," Kendra replied with a grin. "But I

need you to be my doubles partner. Neil is coming over later to play tennis. Call up one of your friends so we'll have a fourth."

"Okay," Lauren agreed cheerfully. She jumped out of bed and dashed toward the bathroom. "Meet you downstairs in twenty minutes."

◆ ◆ ◆

Dinah walked into the breakfast room, looking as glamorous as a character from an old movie. "I'm glad to find you two together," she said, sitting across the table from Kendra and Lauren. "I have something incredible to tell you. I've decided to send you both to school in Switzerland at the start of the new semester. Isn't that exciting! It's a marvelous school—very difficult to get into, but with Graham's connections you've both already been accepted."

Kendra stared at her mother, not believing what she was hearing.

"Now, don't look surprised, Kendra," Dinah went on. "It isn't as if we never talked about your having a year abroad. And you'll be going to one of the very best girls' boarding schools in the world—very advanced. How lucky you are! I wish I'd had such an opportunity when I was your age. Imagine, skiing the Alps—the best teachers . . ."

As her mother rambled on, Kendra tried to contain her anger. How could Dinah spring another change on them like this? Kendra had always hoped to spend a year abroad—but she wanted to talk about it first. Not just have her mother make all the arrangements without even consulting her.

She looked at Lauren to see how she was taking the news. Her sister looked as surprised as Kendra felt.

"Can I bring Vinnie?" Lauren asked.

"Certainly not, but they have horses there—and absolutely everything else—and I'll arrange for you to ride, and we'll make sure that Vinnie is well cared for while you're away."

"I think he'll go nuts without me," Lauren said.

Kendra frowned, remembering the time Vinnie went wild in Central Park and tried to trample Lauren. It had never happened before—and it hadn't happened since. But the fact that her sister had nearly been killed still bothered Kendra.

"Never mind Vinnie," Dinah said impatiently. "Any girl your age would be thrilled at the chance for such an adventure. A year in Switzerland at such a wonderful school. Oh, I know you're going to love it!"

As Lauren began asking questions about the school's stable and the curriculum, Kendra could see her sister was beginning to get excited.

"Will we be living in a huge dormitory, with lots of foreign girls?" Lauren asked.

"Heavens, no!" Dinah exclaimed. "All the girls have their own rooms. I told you, it's a very elegant school—very famous. The students come from all over the world—why, kings and presidents and movie stars all send their daughters there. You'll meet so many interesting people."

"Great," Kendra muttered. All she could think of was how hard it would be to leave Neil.

"This is a great opportunity, Kendra, and you should be thrilled at the chance to see more of the world," Dinah said.

"Do I have a choice?" Kendra said between clenched teeth.

"I think it sounds great, Kennie," Lauren coaxed her. "I love adventures, don't you? And we'll be together, anyhow, so it'll be just like home."

"Not exactly," Kendra told her sister. She turned to Dinah. "When do we leave?"

"In a couple of weeks." Dinah beamed. "Summer's almost over, so we can spend the time shopping and getting you ready."

Kendra crumpled up her napkin and tossed it on the table. Dinah was still chattering to Lauren about the clothes she'd need for Switzerland when Kendra stood up and slipped out the front door.

Neil was just coming up the front path, tennis racquet under his arm. She rushed toward him, and the news about going to school in Switzerland tumbled out even before she said hello.

◆ ◆ ◆

The night air was cool, now that summer was almost over. Kendra had thrown a denim jacket around her shoulders when she and Neil decided to walk around the grounds of the house after dinner.

"Why don't you tell her no—just say that you don't want to go?" Neil asked for the hundredth time. They had spent the whole day together, feeling miserable, and trying to figure out how to convince Dinah to let Kendra stay at home.

She held his hand as they walked along the cliff on the high pathway overlooking the East River. Through the trees lining the path, she could see the lights of bridges and buildings twinkling across the water. Down at the bottom of the sheer drop of the cliff, the lights made wobbly reflections on the rippling water. Under different circumstances, it would have been romantic. But today they were both too depressed to enjoy the view.

"What's up, Kendra? You can usually get your own way with Dinah." Neil continued to press her.

Kendra sighed. "I know, but she seems so determined. She's got everything arranged already, and Lauren seems so excited."

"Maybe Lauren should go by herself. She's old enough to be on her own, and it wouldn't be so bad for her to get away from you for a while."

"Thanks a lot!" Kendra shot back. "I don't want her to have to go alone."

"What about me?" Neil teased her gently. "I'll be alone, too—it'll be horrible. Don't you care?"

She stopped and turned to him. "Of course I do."

Neil smiled and slipped his arms around her. He bent close. She turned her face up to meet his. His kiss was warm and sweet. As they held each other tightly, Kendra felt a terrible sadness. She was truly miserable at the thought of leaving him.

Suddenly, a beautiful sound wafted on the air. It was a soft tinkling song, the music of crystal chimes swaying in a gentle breeze. To Kendra it sounded like music from a dream—strangely familiar, but she couldn't place it. The sound was beautiful, yet haunting. Kendra had the oddest feeling that it was calling to her.

She pulled away from Neil abruptly, trying to listen. But the music was gone.

"What is it?" Neil asked. "You're thinking. Are you going to change your mind?"

"I—I can't Please don't ask me again. You're making me feel worse."

She spun around and stepped out of reach of his arms. Her hair caught on a low hanging branch.

"Ow!" she cried. Kendra struggled to free herself, but her hair had tangled badly on the branch.

"Here, let me."

Neil stepped to the edge of the cliff and reached out. Without warning, the ground under his feet crumbled. He pitched forward over the edge of the cliff and began to plummet down the slope. Tumbling over and over, he plunged down the rocky slide, down toward the water below.

Kendra's eyes opened wide with horror. "Neil!" Her screams filled the air. "Neil!"

While she stood helplessly watching, Neil was falling to his death.

A.G. Cascone

IN A CROOKED LITTLE HOUSE

. . . lived a twisted little man

People are dying at Huntington Prep. A fall down the stairs, a drowning, a fatal bump on the head. It could happen anywhere. But Iggy-Boy knows these aren't accidents. Now he's set his sights on beautiful Casey, the nicest girl in school. She's in terrible danger, but she doesn't know it. She doesn't even know Iggy-Boy exists. But Iggy-Boy is someone she knows, someone nearby, someone who's watching her every move . . .

0-8167-3532-8 • $3.50

WESTWIND